MW01026049

THE MASTER CRAFTSMAN

Other books by Lila Hopkins
From **INGALLS PUBLISHING GROUP, INC**

Weave Me a Song

Strike a Golden Chord

Life is to be embraced and savored!
Lila Hopkins

THE MASTER CRAFTSMAN

by Lila Hopkins

HEARTWARMING NOVEL OF FATHER-SON RELATIONSHIPS
AND THE INCREDIBLE GIFTS OF LOVE

High Country Publishers

INGALLS PUBLISHING GROUP, INC

High Country Publishers book by
INGALLS PUBLISHING GROUP, INC
197 New Market Center, #135
Boone, NC 28607
www.ingallspublishinggroup.com

© 2008 by Lila Hopkins
All rights reserved

Cover painting and illustrations by Lila Hopkins
Cover design by James Geary
Text design by Judy Geary

Library of Congress Cataloging-in-Publication Data

Hopkins, Lila.
The master craftsman : heartwarming novel of father-son
relationships and the incredible gifts of love / by Lila Hopkins.
p. cm.
ISBN-13: 978-1-932158-81-6 (trade pbk. : alk. paper)
1. Fathers and sons--Fiction. I. Title.
PS3558.O63546M37 2008
813'.54--dc22

2007029449

First printing: February 2008

Acknowledgments

Without the help of these fine people, this book could not have been presented to Ingalls Publishing Group:

Cille Dempster, who inspired the story
as her daughter waited for a donor,
Rebecca Loadholt and **Dr. Herman Russell**,
who shared the experience of waiting and receiving,
Amy Warren, who showed me the urgency one feels
in waiting for donor for a loved one,
Joye Russell, who gave me insight into what it's like
to have a loved one receive an organ.

And to:
Becky Sturgill, R.N, who let me be a "patient" at the Dialysis Center at the Fresenius Medical Center in Fuquay-Varina, North Carolina; **Joe Ledford**, who led me to some of the best stone masons in Avery County; **Paul Stroud**, who allowed to quote from his true experience in the Palmico Sound; **Graham Penny** and his **Penny Pickers** for musical inspiration; **Beverle Weller**, who read and proofread and read and proofread again; **Carol** and **Don Flack**, who have served as "first editors" for all my *Fuquay-Independent* columns and now, **The Master Craftsman**.

To **Barbara Ingalls** and **Bob Ingalls**, **Wendy Dingwall**; at Ingalls Publishing Group and especially to **Judy Geary,** my three time book editor! Judy's perseverance in pushing me for accuracy, clarity and depth has made this book what it is.

You are the best!
Lovingly,
Lila Hopkins

Dedication

To all those incredible people
who have given life to one they loved,

Including:
Jim Crissman, who gave a kidney to his brother-in-law,
   Herman Russell in November, 1989 and
Troy Loadholt, who gave a kidney to his mother,
   Becky Loadholt in July, 2002.

And to my friend,
Richard Warren, who continues to wait, with grace.

It is also dedicated to:
the family of Matthew Brown and all those who unselfishly
   donated the organs of a loved one who died too soon.

You have my utmost admiration,
Lila Hopkins

THE MASTER CRAFTSMAN

by Lila Hopkins

Chapter One

A narrow strip of black, wet asphalt, the only space he could delineate in the rain-drenched night, snaked up the dark mountain. It stretched from the hilltop and down into the valley, then up again and another dip – an hypnotic seesaw. The Chevrolet Cavalier surged forward and upward and the thrust felt good.

These were his mountains – where he grew up knowing every peak and fishing stream. Eric Walsh thought of the old Scottish song, "For these are my mountains and I'm coming home." But instead of a singing anticipation, he fought a numbing oppression. *Oh, Kate, if only you were here and could understand my fear.*

The serpentine road would probably make him nauseated, but Eric shifted his weight and leaned toward the window and back again, catching the rhythm of the twisting road – arching, bending – like a rubber raft in white rapids. He was wide-awake now, daring fate and refusing to decrease his speed.

The little dog beside him stirred and whined. Eric took his hand off the steering wheel long enough to touch her. "Hold on, Beast! We'll be at my mom's soon."

He bent his body into another curve. *Shoot*, he thought, I should have rented a sports car in Johnson City! Now that would be the difference in riding in a car and *driving*. He could just imaging a powerful little car hugging these curves. Kate loved sport cars and would have liked to arrive in a

9

sports car convertible – except in this rain. Besides, at six feet, four inches, he was probably too big for a smaller car.

But then, Kate wasn't with him. "Perhaps I'll join you later," she had said. "I planned this trip months ago. My family is expecting me to be there for Julie's graduation."

The speed had been exhilarating, but it failed to lift his depression. He eased off the accelerator and a terrible emptiness enveloped him. He elbowed the dog to wake her up. "How about our calling Kate?" The Shih Tzu sat up and nudged his arm. He pulled his cell phone out of its case and, using his thumb, punched in Kate's number.

All he heard was static from the mountains and the weather. He glanced at the clock, glowing a blueish-green on the dashboard. It was nearly midnight. Just as well he hadn't reached her. He would have to confess that he had broken his promise to stop for the night in Johnson City. "Oh well, we would just worry her."

The dog's ears popped up, and she twisted her head to give Eric an inquisitive glance. "You know, hound, you are pretty good to talk to. No cautioning me to take care of myself and no nagging." His voice wavered like the phone static. Eric was surprised at the weariness he heard in his own voice.

The dog sat up and gently nosed Eric's hand as if she too wanted the pain to go away.

Eric shoved the phone back into its case. He let his hand linger on the dog's small warm body, and, strangely, it was a comfort to him to have her with him. "We don't need to fret. The dialysis support group warned me of mood changes, little friend. I'm okay. I suppose."

Out of the dark forest a deer ran onto the highway, and Eric struggled for control as the car skidded across the road. He felt a sharp *plunk* as he shoved down on the brakes; he glanced into the rearview mirror and saw a doe falling to her knees, then leaping up. He had only grazed her, thank God.

The car skidded onto the gravel shoulder and came to a shuddering halt just beyond a guard rail. Eric glanced back at the highway, realizing he had neither passed nor met a vehicle since he left Hampton.

As he opened the door, he heard the clinking sound of rocks falling along the trail and knew the deer had made it down the side of the mountain.

A sudden lull in the storm brought the scent of ozone. Eric took a deep breath. He and the dog were the solitary travelers because sensible people were smart enough to stay out of the storm. Sulfurous lightning and the murky gloom created an eerie surrealism

The bleakness of the mountains mirrored his own melancholy. *We have never quarreled before, Kate. I know it hasn't been easy, yet in the early stages of my illness, you supported me with a love to make any man strong.* What had happened to their marriage? He could trace it back to the day Clay came running into the house. "Dad, Mom! I'm a perfect match!"

Eric crossed his arms on the steering wheel and rested his head on them. The idea of Clay being a kidney donor for him was out of the question. He wouldn't allow it, nor would Dr. Young – if his fear about the family history proved true.

The only sounds he heard were the dripping water and an occasional clap of thunder. The feeling of loneliness wasn't new to him, but this time it carried an ominous foreboding of permanence.

Since his quarrel with Kate – the sustaining love of his life – he was being stalked by the sinister isolation of his grim choice. He pounded his fists on the steering wheel. *I cannot endanger Clay.* Life wouldn't be worth living if it cost the life of my son. *I just cannot do it, Kate. I'll die first.* Clay had quoted Dr. Young, "The preliminary tests show a remarkable compatibility."

As he stepped slowly out of the car to inspect it for damage, the rain intensified. Eric moved, head bent against the storm, to the trunk to get a flashlight and umbrella. Finding no damage that he could see in the rain, he started around to the passenger side – but there was no room to walk. Indeed, during a flash of lightning, he saw the right front tire, slowing its spin, hanging into space.

Eric leaned against the car. Another few inches and he would have been airborne. He glanced across the black canyon but he instead of a prayer of relief; he voiced stinging regret. It would have been such an easy escape.

He shuffled back around the car. When he opened the driver's door, the Shih Tzu scurried by him and dashed into the dark. "Dumb dog! You get all messed up and I'll have to answer to Kate *and* my mother!" Eric yelled as he dropped into the seat.

He could excuse a dog, but he had been the dumb one. He should never use a phone while driving and he had already broken a promise to his wife since he hadn't stopped for the night. But, he reasoned, he was less than seventy miles from home.

He should have let his brother Joel to meet him at the Tri-City Airport.

He grabbed the door handle to haul himself out of the car to go look for the dog, but she waited patiently by the door– a little wet cream-colored mop, her tiny, flat face lifted up expectantly. He reached under the dog's middle, lifted her, again surprised by her weight. He brushed more water off his soaked knees. "You are pitiful; do you know that? And you got your pink ribbon wet. How in heaven's name am I going to tie a new ribbon on you?" The dog answered with a throaty, chortling reprimand.

"Hush, Beast. You smell like a wet dog." He raised his hand to ward off imaginary blows. "Don't clobber me, Kate! I know about all that expensive 'flower smelling' dog shampoo you buy."

To the dog, he said, "I didn't mean it, Beast. You smell – well, you do smell like a wet dog, but I like it."

The dog cocked her head to stare at him. She offered a tenuous, growled complaint. Then, apparently reassured, she lay down, smuggling close to his leg.

"Well, good, a truce. I hope you know, little one, how much Kate hates to give you up – but she promised you to Mom. She said Mom needed you more."

Kate's eyes had filled with tears when she put the dog in her crate for the taxi ride to the airport.. "Honey, if you love her so much, keep her and we'll get another one for Mom," Eric said.

"No. I trained her for your mom. It would take time to find and train another dog, and ... you just never know ..."

He eased the car backward into the road and stepped on the gas. He wouldn't tell Kate anything about this night. Kate seemed preoccupied about death lately. They were all getting sick of dialysis clinics. He understood Kate's depression, but she didn't help his misery when, at La Guardia, she boarded a flight for Kentucky to her niece's graduation just minutes before his plane left for Tennessee. He suspected she wanted to forget about the clinics for a few days, and he guessed she needed a little relief.

The thought of the dialysis clinics made him think of his son Clay, and he felt wretched, suddenly too tired to go on to North Carolina. The curves he had just maneuvered were nothing compared to the switchback turns in Avery County, and he had better stop driving while he was still alert – at least partially alert.

He couldn't rouse the night watchman in the first motel but stopped at the next, a small rustic place that he would never have stopped at had Kate been with him. The attendant came to the door, shoving his shirttail into his trousers. His tousled hair made him look like the dog Eric cradled in his right arm. He had caught the dog in another escape attempt and forgot he still held her.

The sleepy-eyed man studied Eric's wet blond hair and slowly brought his eyes down to rest on his damp clothing.

Eric knew he must look dead tired and guessed he had dark

circles around his eyes from fatigue. Irritated, Eric leaned toward him and whispered, "It's raining corpses and dogs."

The clerk jumped back a step and stuttered, "Oh, no, sir. I didn't know it was raining that hard. I was just thinking – as skinny as you are – you would have to stand twice to cast a shadow."

Eric laughed. He was used to corny jokes about his height, but hadn't heard one about his build – but he had never been this thin before. "Sorry to be so late tonight," he said.

"Actually ... you're early." The clerk gazed at the clock above the desk that registered 1:05.

"Or early," Eric repeated, also gazing at the clock. Perhaps he could squeeze in four or five hours of sleep.

Pointing to the dog, the man said, "Is that thang real? Looks like a toy. I'll have to charge more for a dog – owner's orders."

"Okay. I understand. She's a belated gift to my mother for her 84th birthday. Wanted a lap dog."

"Wal, she sure ain't no sheep dog! She housebroke?" He giggled like an embarrassed teenager. "The dog, I mean."

"They both are," Eric said, deadpan.

"Then, fergit the extra charge. For the dog, I mean." He scrunched up his eyes trying to read the name on Eric's credit card. "Thank you, Mr. String, er, ah, Mr. Walsh.."

Eric was too tired to appreciate this latest attempt at humor. He pulled his traveling case down the hall to the room and flipped on the light. He fell across the bed, then turned on the radio. It was set on a country music station and he lay silent, listening. "Amazing," he said to the dog. His own brother Joel was serenading him on the country station.

"Life is like a mountain railroad, with an engineer that's brave ..." Joel sang.

Eric listened to the end of the song.

"Keep your hand upon the throttle, and your eye upon the road," Joel concluded.

Eric hadn't kept his eye on the road very well tonight, nor was he brave. He breathed a prayer that the doe he hit was all right and turned off the radio. Joel had always wanted to be a singer. Five years Eric's senior, he left home when Eric was 13 and climbed quickly to success, first in a Nashville band and then in The Grand Ole Opry.

***

Eric came home from high school when he was fifteen to see the white lace tablecloth and his mother's best china on the dining room table. His younger sister Betsy explained that neighbors were coming to dinner to watch the television show with them. "Do you think they will do a closeup of Joel?"

"If he has a solo, they probably will. Does Joel have a solo?"

"Yes, yes, yes! His first national show!"

When their mother announced supper, the mouth-watering aroma of country ham and spicy stewed apples beckoned them to the table. Pastor Earl, a retired minister, gave the blessing in his rich, baritone voice that revealed an obvious familiarity with the Deity. "My dear wife used to fix apples like these," he remarked and scooped spoonfuls of the cinnamon flavored fruit onto his plate.

The family tried to talk about news other than the Nashville Television Special; it was just too exciting for dinner-table conversation, his father insisted. Betsy and her grandmother were already hyper-active. Brother Earl tried to keep the conversation relevant. "I took a long hike up to where my great grandparents had a little cabin. There's nothing left of the structure since even the logs have rotted. The old chimney is standing, though. Nothing left of the cabin, only the gray stones."

"Did you ever leave the mountains, Pastor Earl?" Betsy asked in her high-pitched voice.

The old man laid down his fork. He pulled on the white beard, smoothing it down the way Eric had seen him do so many times. "You mean leave not planning to come back?" He reared back in his chair, white eyebrows pulled way up over wide eyes. "Never! I did leave once, though, for awhile. Got my college degree and served my country in the navy, but I couldn't wait to come home. I came back to marry my girl and to work in my Blue Ridge Mountains. I will paraphrase the old saying, You can take a boy out of the mountains, but you can't take the mountains out of the boy."

Then Pastor Earl turned the conversation to Eric. "I see you're making progress on the stone wall. Are you also working on a new painting?"

Eric's dad replied, "The boy should have been his grandfather's son. He's the kind of son my father always wanted. One who could draw pictures."

Grandma clucked softly. "Now, now, son."

Before Eric had a chance to tell Brother Earl about his new work, they moved to the living room and Betsy found a place on the floor directly in front of the television set. Grandma pulled her rocking chair up as close to the screen as she could and not block the view for others. Expectancy filled the room.

The Nashville Special was more than half over before they announced Joel's number.

Betsy gave a squeal of joy when Joel stepped lightly to the microphone. The band played a harmonious introduction as Joel began to strum his guitar, and for all the world, it was as though he was right there in their little living room. Eric caught his breath as his brother began to sing his own composition, "Mountain Glory."

Joel closed his eyes and a strand of dark hair slid down on his forehead, accentuating his youth. The cameras captured the wistful homesickness in the face of the lad as he sang of blue mountains. The music was full of emotion, flowing and sweet sounding, and it was as though he was singing only for his family. Twice, the camera broke away to focus on a panorama of snow covered mountain peaks then panned back to Joel, catching the motion of the lock of dark hair swaying back and forth in rhythm with the melody. His home audience sat absolutely still, hypnotized, straining to hold on to every word, eyes glued to the singer. Eric felt goose-pimples on his arms.

Before Joel was introduced, Eric noticed that his father had slipped from his seat to stand behind them to watch his son perform on television. He stood mute, arms folded across his chest. When the song was over, Eric saw unmistakable pride in his father's face. But the sarcasm in his voice was like a flick of a whip across Eric's face. "One and a half minutes of glory." He stomped from

16

the room and the floor vibrated as he walked across the porch and down the stairs.

For a while no one else said a word. Even though a different musical ensemble occupied the television screen, Joel's song seemed to linger in the room, like the fragrance of sweet honeysuckle on a warm day. Eric's chest hurt, like your heart could really ache from missing someone. He had almost forgotten how Joel looked and how much his eyes and hair were like their father's. He tried to lock in the memory of Joel's voice so he wouldn't forget it. "Like a dulcimer," his grandpa had said, but Eric knew Joel's voice had a lot more richness to it. It had grown deeper in the years he had been away.

Eric's mother touched Pastor Earl's arm as he was leaving. "Don't mind my husband. He just misses his sons. Ed and Joel have already left, and I suppose Eric will leave the mountains eventually. Albert always thought they would remain near us and he could have a similar relationship with them that he had with *his* father."

***

Eric felt sick in the pit of his stomach. He had heard that a person facing imminent death often sees his life flash before him, but did he have to experience the same raw emotions he had known before? He had worked all his life to develop a relationship with his dad, but he wondered if his father had ever missed him after he left home. His life had been defined by his relationship with his father, and now he was faced with a decision that could destroy his relationship with *his* son.

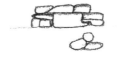

Chapter Two

He woke up early, gave the dog her outside break; then he sprawled back across the bed for a few minutes. He woke up again when the sun was shining brightly. He sat up and rubbed his weary eyes. He had often been apprehensive about family reunions, but on this trip he hoped to find the wisdom he needed to make the right decision. His mother knew he was on dialysis, but he had not shared the severity of his illness with her. He suspected that Kate had talked with Joel and Sherie about Clay's offer, but he wanted to talk to his mother. She might know more about the details of Grandpa's death than he did.

He opened a bag of dried food, and the dog gave him an offended look and retreated to sit under a chair. "Look, Beast, I can't carry an open can in the car and you wouldn't finish a can."

The Shih Tzu stared at him. She lifted one paw and her round brown eyes were pleading. "You are so very pathetic," he snorted. "You and your pushed-in nose." She looked at him sorrowfully and then reluctantly walked to the food and tasted it. She wrinkled her flat, fuzzy face and spat out some. When he made no attempt to serve her anything else, she ate a few bites, ever so slowly, pausing at intervals to see if he was watching.

He prepared the instant hot coffee the motel supplied and hurried to get things ready to leave. Kate had packed all his medicine, sorted by day into weekly pill boxes. With a smile of anticipation, he looked for what he knew would be there also – a chocolate mint for each day he planned to be gone. Every bag she had packed for him during the last thirty years had included chocolate mints – like the ones that were on their hotel pillows each night of their honeymoon. *Thank God for Kate*, he thought. Without her, he would have given up the long wait for a kidney.

Anyone's feet can swell while traveling, he told himself as he worked his toes into his loafers. The shirt he had worn the evening before was dry, so he shoved it into his carry-on bag. He would wait until he got home to shower and shave.

Home. He knew his mother would be counting the minutes until he arrived, but she was uncanny in her perceptions. He'd have to be careful when they talked about Kate. Hopefully, she'd be so excited about the mutt, she wouldn't think to press him for details. Kate had called the dog Baby, and he used a variety of names from Beast to some he wouldn't say in front of his mother. He had to admit that he had grown fond of the little critter, even if she seemed to only tolerate him. She had a happy disposition and seemed fearless, even with bigger dogs. Until he had spent time with her, he had insisted he had no use for little lap dogs. Give him a cross-breed cur anytime. His boyhood dog, Soccer had no pedigree papers and certainly needed no daily hair brushing, but he was a great pet.

Joel and his wife, Sherie, had moved in with his mother to provide the care she needed. They had converted two large bedrooms into a tidy apartment for her. She could cook as she liked or take all her meals with them. When they were on tour, their sister Betsy looked after their mother. He shoved aside the old guilty feelings he had because he had been unable to come home to help care for either her or their father. But, he reminded himself, he had supplied the money to renovate the house. He and Kate. She had been the instigator. "We helped my mom keep her home. We need to help your mother," she said.

Betsy and her soft-spoken husband Russell had taken over their grandparent's place and turned it into a Bed and Breakfast. Kate and Eric were part owners, and he was eager to see what Betsy had done with it. Betsy and Russell had a brood of four sons, and he was eager to see how they had grown. Would they be like his father and grandfather – products of these mountains?

Joel and Sherie had a couple of grown daughters. Eric hadn't seen them in years. He had been remiss in keeping up with his family.

He filled his lungs with glorious, fresh mountain air. No city ever smelled like this! For just a little while, he felt glad to be alive. Perhaps his depression last night was due to the storm.

Yesterday's rain had left everything green, looking fresh and new – just the way he loved the mountains best. No wonder some of the first settlers were from Scotland. He could almost hear Scottish bagpipes and again words from his favorite song came to him. "For these are my mountains, and this is my glen. The place of my childhood will know me again."

He turned to the east to Grandfather Mountain. From some directions it looked like the profile of an old man, hence its name. But from Banner Elk and Walsh Mountain he could see the rugged peaks. From each angle it showed a different face, making it especially challenging to an artist.

"I'd love to go horseback riding," he said to the dog. What a strange wish. He had never been fond of horseback riding. Kate was the equestrian in the family.

He had intended to stop for breakfast, but once in the car, he headed straight past Roan Mountain and on through Banner Elk. At the foot of Walsh Mountain, he pulled off at an overlook to get the dog ready. Kate had typed out specific instructions. As he got out of the car, he realized instinct had led him to a familiar spot. He had painted this scene many times, but always wanted to do it again. The canvas couldn't do justice to the hardwood-covered mountain crowned by boulders. When he showed the height of the peak, he lost the sense of space he wanted in the sky. Today the huge granite boulders looked like they had been whitewashed in the early light. The cloudless sky was a clear cerulean blue. This was Walsh Mountain. His legacy.

"Well, girl, it's just you and me." The Shih Tzu watched him nervously when he lifted her to her blanket on the hood of the car. The rain-saturated pink ribbon on her head gave no resistance when he tugged. "Now how in heaven's name am I supposed to brush your hair and tie a ribbon to it?"

Years ago, when Kate was away for a few days, he had to get their first grader, Kathy ready for school. She finally grabbed the brush from him and insisted on doing it herself. Eric timidly held up the longer hair from the back of the dog's neck. He had seen Kate do it a thousand times. He pulled out her instructions from his shirt pocket. "Brush top hair in layers."

Layers? Using the brush Kate had supplied, he swiped at the long soft cream-colored hair. "Part hair on back so it falls evenly on both sides of the dog." He accomplished that rather professionally, he thought. He knew he could never get a rubber band and ribbon on her longer head hair, but he drew his fingers into a claw and brushed at the "pony tail."

His masculine skills did not include grooming a fake-looking toy dog. "You look kind of scruffy, rather like a scare-crow, but it will have to do."

He set her on the ground and was disgusted when she raced to the wet grass to roll over and over. Then, she had a good laugh on him. After a good shake, the coat fell into its natural pattern, parting in the middle and draping over her sides.

"So, what did you need me for?"

He had been instructed to present the dog in the carrying crate,

21

with the big pink ribbon on it so he put her in it. "You are rather comical and full of your own importance, but I suspect my mother will be crazy about you."

***

In spite of his fatigue, his heart was pounding with excitement when he pulled up to the front of the house. Joel came running from his studio at the back and Joel's wife Sherie hurried down the front steps, beating Joel to him. He thought she was one of the prettiest ladies he had ever known and he would usually swing her around in his arms, but couldn't manage that this morning – before breakfast, as he explained to her.

Joel gripped his hand, "Welcome home, little brother."

"Hello, *little* brother. Where did all this gray hair come from?"

"I'm an old man. Nearly sixty, you know."

Their father had also had prematurely gray hair. He looked so much like their father that Eric almost expected Joel to jump on him for some mistake he had made.

"Where's the puppy?" Sherie asked and then let out a squeal of delight when she saw the dog looking out mournfully from the crate. In her jeans and a tee shirt, she looked and sounded like a teenager. "Come, little one, let Sherie fix you some breakfast."

"Hey," Eric said, "she's eaten. I haven't."

"We'll take care of both of you."

His mother met him on the porch, and her hug lacked the strength of her earlier years. So did his. As usual, his mother was groomed like she was expecting company, in pressed tan slacks and a pressed pink blouse. She had a regal aura about her which he had never seen in another lady, until he met Kate. She had grown up with few luxuries and worked hard keeping house for four children and a stone mason whose clothes and boots were covered in mortar, yet Eric thought she presented the picture of elegance and beauty. He found himself trying to explain why Kate wasn't with him. "Her favorite niece is graduating from high school, and she felt she had to be there. She'll come on down here after she visits her family."

"Of course," his mother said but she studied his eyes a little too long. "You look really tired. Kate called last night. I think she thought you might have tried to drive straight through and she was worried. She wanted to let us all know she had a safe trip to her mother's home."

"She called? Good. She was determined you have this as soon as possible." Eric offered the empty crate, then indicated the puppy in Sherie's arms. "I'm sorry we're about two weeks late for your birthday."

"I plan to call her Princess," she said, taking the Shih Tzu from Sherie. "Come to me little, darling. Betsy and I have been reading a library book about her breed."

Joel reached in the car for his bag. "Come on into the house!"

Chapter Three

Eric followed Sherie and his mother – still holding the dog – into the living room.

"It looks just like it always has!" he exclaimed. The sun from the open door showed the familiar, comfortable furniture.

"Still with the frayed couch," his mother said quietly.

"But it's comfortable and it's home, Mom." He gave her a hug and petted the head of the dog. He stepped closer to the massive fireplace, crafted by his dad. He ran his hand over the cool, hard granite. "We chopped many a log for use in here, eh, Joel? I can almost feel the yellow and blue flames on a cold winter day."

He glanced around. Every wall – living room and the hallway – held his paintings. "Why do you plaster my pictures everywhere? Can't you afford any good work?"

"Watch it, mister," Mom bristled. "These are works of my favorite artist, and that one over the fireplace hung in the governor's mansion in Raleigh for more than ten years." Her voice grew softer. "Your dad loved that picture, son."

Eric raised his eyes to the painting he had done in high school. He reached up to touch the glass-protected image of his grandfather, standing near his father. He said, "They died too soon. Both –" Tears welled up and he dragged his forearm across his face as he reached up to trace the scaffold that supported his dad. He swallowed hard, the lump in his throat rose and fell, but it didn't dissipate. "Both of them did."

Eric's cleared his throat. "I wonder if either could have lived longer with today's advances in medicine." He was only thirteen when his grandfather died of kidney failure.

His father might have lived with a heart transplant, but he probably would have rejected such an idea. He had needed several blood transfusions as a result of a bleeding ulcer while Eric was still in school and his children wanted to donate blood to the blood bank to replace it.

"Absolutely, no!" his father barked. And that was the end of it. Now Eric wished he had asked him why.

"Obstinate, bullheaded," Eric muttered.

"What did you say?" Mom asked.

"I was talking about when I painted that."

Joel put his hand on his shoulder and Eric knew he had heard him. "I can smell the coffee, Eric."

They heard someone running up the front stairs and he turned to welcome his sister Betsy. She clung to him longer than usual. "You okay?" she asked. "Oh, here is the puppy!" Mom passed the dog to Betsy who squealed with delight at the tiny wet tongue kissing her face.

He never understood brothers and sisters who fought with each other. He and Betsy were as close as "two peas in a pod" as his grandma used to say. Four years ago she sent him flowers and a sympathy card on his fiftieth birthday. She would be fifty next spring and he could hardly wait to return the favor. They were younger than Ed and Joel, they remained at home long after the older brothers left. They didn't always agree, but let someone jump on one, and he would have two to whip. With her blond hair tied in a pony tail, and wearing a cotton tee shirt and jeans, she looked like

25

the teenager she was when he first left home.

Now she stared at him anxiously. When he walked on toward the kitchen, she relaxed. "Oh, I need to tell you that you can't stay at the Bed and Breakfast just yet. I had a chance to rent the entire house for a family reunion. They will be gone before Kate comes, so you can have it then."

"My old room will be fine. I don't know when Kate will arrive, but I want to be near Mom anyway. Is my old room okay?" he called to Sherie.

"Of course, but please come eat. Eggs and toast?" He'd shared some of the restrictions in his diet when he told them he was coming.

"Just coffee."

"Not on your life," his mother insisted. "Kate said we were to be sure that you ate your meals, especially breakfast."

"What is all this?" Eric laughed with pleasure when he spotted the bed and paraphernalia his mom had collected for Princess. "Why did you buy all these toys? Kate sent some of the dog's favorites. You didn't have to buy more."

His mother retrieved the small dog from Betsy. "My friends gave me a 'puppy shower.' Where did Kate find her?"

"She wrote a book about the breed; I didn't illustrate it. They used photographs," he explained. "I brought you a copy. Kate became friends with the breeder."

"I'm sure she hated to give her up!"

"Yes. But you know Kate. She has a house full of pets. Kathy is probably looking for a new one now. Sometimes people just drop off injured or abandoned pets at the vet's."

"As soon as you eat, we need to look at the B&B before the other family arrives," Betsy said.

"Wait, Betsy," their mom said. "I need to hear about my grandchildren."

"And your great grandchildren? Everyone is fine, Mom. Kathy loves the veterinary clinic where she works. She and Paul are expecting their first child. Clay and Jane and Tim and Valerie are doing great. Tim wants to become an Olympic runner. Every time I see him he wants me to *run* with him."

***

The two homes were built at a friendly angle, as though they were Victorian ladies nodding at each other. They were built on a crest, just below the incline that led to the peak of Walsh's Stone Mountain, named that because of the beautiful granite found on it, some with flecks of mica. There was a peaceful symmetry in the arrangement. They were not identical – his grandparents' house was older and slightly smaller – but they complemented each other.

Each featured an inviting wrap-a-round porch, steep roofs and large shutters. The grandparents' house had four bedrooms, while Eric's parents' house had four bedrooms upstairs and two downstairs. Betsy bubbled with excitement as she told him about painting the shutters and trim on the bed and breakfast by herself.

Betsy and his daughter, Kathy, were very much alike – in appearance as well as interests. His daughter, like his sister, had always wanted to become a veterinarian. Each had the ability to remain "focused" on tasks until they were finished. Betsy, however, had chosen an early marriage over a career.

"I really like the gray for the B&B. You didn't do all of that did you?"

"Russell and the boys helped. Joel hired them to paint Mom's."

From the front of the building, Eric could see that she had done a lot of work. A laser-cut, wooden sign identified it.

Rhododendron Bed and Breakfast
Betsy and Russell Adams
Proprietors

"Sorry, there was no room to list the owners." Betsy seemed embarrassed.

"There is no need to list the owners."

She put her arm around his waist and they walked up the steps.

Inside the bed and breakfast, the massive fireplace in the parlor was handcrafted by their grandfather. His unique brush strokes were large stones with glittering flecks of mica, fit so exactly that the mortar hardly showed.

This house featured a smaller living room, or parlor, as Grandmother had insisted on calling it, and a small dining room but a huge kitchen that was built across the back of the house. One end featured another signature fireplace and sitting space that made it the family room.

Eric inspected each fireplace and the foundation of the house, also built with stones. "I see you have had some repairs done. Where did you find such a capable mason?"

Betsy smiled. "Well, we considered sending for Clay ... Then you'll never guess who showed up! Remember your old nemesis, Durrell?"

"I couldn't forget Durrell, unfortunately. Do you mean he did all this work?" Eric whistled. "I ought to look him up."

"You won't have to. He's eager to see you and will drop by one afternoon. By the way, I'll take you to Boone tomorrow."

"That's not necessary. You're too busy here. I can drive to the clinic and I'll be there for hours. Fortunately, the treatments have never made me nauseated and have only rarely given me a headache"

"I have lots of shopping to do in Boone for the B&B guests. I won't have much time for the next week – and I really want to spend some time with you. I can stay with you some of the time you are getting the treatment, can't I?"

"I'm afraid not. No visitors. Germ control – no offense! But if you take me you'll have to wait in the chilly lobby. Bring a sweater and a good book. They keep the rooms at a steady seventy-two degrees."

Betsy laughed. "This is the mountains, remember. Seventy degrees is high noon in July." She hugged him again. "Don't worry about me. I'll drop you off and be waiting when you're finished."

He surveyed the yard, shading his eyes so she couldn't see how misty-eyed he'd gotten. "I see that you didn't leave much for me to help with."

"Oh, but I did! You know your wall? I want it extended around the old apple tree."

After an involuntary gasp, he laughed. "I'm not quite up to

that, I'm afraid, but we might get Clay up here. I gave him the tools that Grandpa used that Dad gave me."

Betsy was serious when she said, "You know there is plenty of space to build an artist's studio. It could be near Joel's recording studio, just beyond Dad's tool shed."

Eric shielded his eyes with his hand. "I can see it now – a whole cluster of unlikely studios behind the houses. We could build one for every member of the family."

***

After dinner they took their coffee cups to the front porch. As soon as Eric chose one of the six old rocking chairs, Princess began bounding about on her hind legs, front paws waving above her head. Eric was surprised. "Why you little trickster. You have never begged for me before. You wait until I have a cup of hot coffee and then ask me to hold you." He leaned over to place his cup on the porch rail, and swooped the dog into his arms. "Would you believe this little mutt weighs nearly fifteen pounds? She's as small as a gray squirrel but she is a sturdy little dog."

Joel handed him his cup. "Eric, I can take you to town tomorrow. The clinic called today while you were with Betsy to confirm your appointment."

"Bets insists on taking me. I'm perfectly capable of driving. I drive everywhere, and the treatments have never made me sick."

Sherie said, "It seems to me that you do just about everything you want to do."

"I don't want to build another stone wall," he said. Then he smiled. "But I surely wish I had the energy to do that kind of a job again."

"We all wish for the energy we had as kids – just not the chores." Joel ran his hands through his gray hair. A soft flutter of laughter rippled across the porch.

Eric breathed in the familiar fragrance of the pines and junipers. Late-dining hummingbirds fed at the red hibiscus in a clay pot near on the top step. As daylight faded, the tree frogs began the evening serenade. The peacefulness of the mountains seeped though his bones and he leaned back and stretched his legs out.

His mom touched his knee. "Does it hurt, son? You know – that treatment you get?" She twisted her fingers together indicating that she was uneasy talking about the subject.

"Dialysis? No, it doesn't hurt. But, it's so time consuming. At least four hours, three days a week. It rules my life, but since my kidneys are functioning at about twenty per cent, it's necessary."

Sherie walked across the porch, serving fresh coffee. "Show me the catheter. I'm good at changing bandages."

When Eric shifted his weight, Princess jumped down and turned to rebuke him with a haughty stare. His mother called the dog to sit with her. "I have a better lap, anyway," she insisted. "And I'm your new owner now."

Eric stood up and unbuttoned his shirt. "Are you sure you want to see my war wounds? I don't have a catheter now. ... It's been replaced with a port called a fistula.." He pulled the shirt from his pants and showed them the little scar on his left shoulder. "I had a temporary catheter here, but they put the fistula in my – what they called 'non-dominant' arm. That gives me my right arm freer to work with. See? Right here." He pointed to the fistula just above the bend of his left elbow. "I wear long sleeves to protect it. They join an artery to a vein, giving access to my blood vessels." He shoved his shirt back into his pants and sat down to button it.

"I didn't mean to embarrass you," Sherie said. "I know your modesty is important. I was a nurse when I met Joel."

"Someone who has been through all this tends to lose a lot of their sense of modesty." He sighed. They had been skirting around his problem all day. Now it was out in the open, where they could acknowledge it and talk frankly about it. He just didn't know how to tell his mother that he had been diagnosed with end stage renal disease.

His mother said, "I have never understood why you needed dialysis and exactly what it does."

"My kidneys function only at twenty percent of their capacity. Sometimes only fifteen per cent."

"Dialysis cleans the blood, just like your kidneys do," Sherie said.

"It removes salt and wastes as well as excess water from the blood."

"Yes," Eric said. "It also keeps a safe level of certain chemicals and helps to control high blood pressure." He sighed. "My biggest problem is fatigue. I have to rest during the day and I go to bed disgustingly early."

"You and Mom!" Joel said. "She goes to bed at dark."

"And speaking of which. ..." Their mother laughed and stood up. "I hate to go so early on your first evening home, but, I have to say goodnight."

Eric stood up to kiss his mother and returned to sit with Joel and Sherie.

Joel asked quietly, "In the event that a kidney becomes available, how long do doctor's have to transplant it?"

"It sounds strange, but they call it – the time an organ can be held before transplantation – the 'shelf life.' For a kidney. the maximum time is 72 hours. Much shorter for heart and lungs. After this trip, I won't dare leave New York for fear of losing my chance in line for a kidney."

"By the way, Eric. I got the copy of Grandpa's death certificate that you asked for. It says he died with kidney failure caused by diabetes."

"At least that doesn't indicate that renal disease runs in our family. Thanks, Joel. I'll take a copy to Dr. Young."

***

After he left them, he could hear the quiet voices of Joel and Sherie still on the porch. The sound was soothing and restful. He picked up his cell phone from its recharging base and punched in Kate's number. She didn't answer her phone, but he shouldn't be

31

surprised. She was probably at some graduation celebration. He got ready for bed, but left the phone on the night stand beside his head in case she saw him on caller ID and returned his call late. The swelling in his feet and legs made him awkward, so he sat on the edge of the bed and lifted his legs in with his hands.

He watched the phone.

On their very first date, as soon as they were seated in the small booth in a Chinese restaurant in Chicago she asked, "Why are you an artist?"

"Why?" he repeated, stalling for time. "It's a compulsion – like 'an itch I can't scratch.' No, that's not it. That's a definition for love I read somewhere, and not a very good one."

"It's not a good definition for why you are an artist *or* for love."

He spread out his long fingers. "No one ever asked me that question. I'm an artist because it's something I have to do. I don't know if I can explain. It's a craving I need to satisfy. I'm happiest when I am at work with a brush."

She smiled. "Are you any good?"

"Well, ... I am good," he said grinning. "At least Grandpa said I was, but I need instruction. That's why I am at the Art Institute. Was that going to be your next question?"

She giggled and he relaxed. "Okay, what is *your* definition of love?"

"*My* definition? I don't suppose I have ever been in love." He gave it a stab. "I think love would involve being completely wrapped up with another person – excited by them and wanting only what's best for them. Putting that person first."

"And, wanting to be with that someone all the time. It carries the responsibility of complete fidelity. " She twisted her school ring.

"Love, to me, should be enduring!" he said, and they laughed because they noticed an older couple seated in the table next to them listening and nodding.

"Now, we have settled all that and come up with a conclusive definition of love. Let's move on to something else."

"Okay." Eric wondered why her cheeks were suddenly pink.

Tonight he thought of Kate. "Putting that person first," he had said. But he had refused to go to her mother's home before coming here. *Darling, I simply did not have the energy and couldn't face another delay to find if I have made the right decision. I also knew I had to get to the clinic for treatment. I wish you understood.* But why had he not told her that?

Chapter Four

He spent the night tossing and turning, and dreaming of the time that, *Please, God*, he would get a call to report to the hospital immediately for surgery. How long would he have to wait for the kidney? He knew of several patients who had been waiting for years, but he didn't have that long.

He loved being in his old room, but he had forgotten about how small the bed was and as he curled up to accommodate for the size, he longed for Kate. He wouldn't mind the too small bed, if he could curl around his wife. She was a pretty tall girl and they would need a longer bed if she ever came to sleep with him. The beds in the B&B were queen-sized and a room would surely be available by then.

He turned over again. Boyhood memories, not all of them good, played through his mind, especially an experience when he was fifteen. He stirred in the short bed. The action played in his mind in accurate, perfect sequence.

***

It was the first summer working day and his dad had hired him to work on his crew. At the noon break, he pulled out his sketching pad and walked to the edge of the woods to eat his lunch and to draw. He drew the cougar he had studied at

the Grandfather Mountain Animal Habitat the week before.

With golden eyes the size of golf balls, the cougar stared at him. The big cat flattened his ears and dropped his belly low to the boulder. Twitching a tail that was as thick as the boy's fist and as long as the animal's sleek body, the big cat waited. Muscles in his powerful shoulders rippled in a smooth flow of motion that caught the sunlight. The gloss of his reddish coat held the boy's attention and he sketched quickly. The cat paused on his haunches, and the soft pads on his feet gripped the granite as he poised to leap. Eric added whiskers with swift, firm strokes.

Then, his father stepped out of the woods. He angrily grabbed the boy's shoulder and Eric yelled in surprise, knocking his sketchbook to the ground and scattering his pencils and his uneaten lunch.

"So this is the kind of worker you turn out to be. You sit here while I fight a tight schedule ."

"But, it's my lunch break, Dad."

"It's two o'clock"

Eric's face contorted with pain and embarrassment. "I lost track of the time. I'm sorry." His insides twisted and his empty stomach drew into a hard knot as he dropped to his knees to retrieve his supplies. But his father was already gone, and so was his vivid image of the cougar.

Eric could hear branches and twigs cracking as his dad headed back to the building site.

Trouble with drawing was, as his mother often pointed out, it just carried Eric away. It gave him wings and he could *soar*; he could forget about Joel being gone and Grandpa and the whole dumb work problem while he was drawing. But the reality was that he had failed his dad. Failed miserably.

He felt sick at heart as he hurried after his father. He *knew* they were on a tight working schedule and had experienced many delays because of the harsh weather, of the past winter.

As he stumbled through the brush, his jacket caught on tree limbs, slowing him. Finally, he removed his jacket and laid it on the ground. He dropped his art materials in the middle and wadded up his drawings into hard little balls and threw them on top.

He folded the tail of the jacket and knotted the sleeves around the middle to form a pack. His hands botched the job and he had to start again. So angry was he with himself that he felt like kicking the pack all the way back to the work site.

His nose was running and he sniffled loudly. He stretched his facial muscles, opening his mouth, yawning, straining to keep the skin around his eyes taut to discourage tears. *He would not cry.* He brushed moisture from each cheek with the back of his hand.

He was startled to see how high his dad's scaffold had been raised and several fresh courses of stones added to the chimney. Before his lunch break he had been serving as his father's helper. Now he saw that he had been replaced by Durrell.

Old Mike was shoveling another load of mortar into the buckets. If he could have just slipped quietly by the crew and ducked into the truck, he would have. But Mike saw him, and the fatigue in the older man's face made Eric cringe. He dropped his pack and reached for the hose. to clean the mixer. He was grateful that Mike was manning the mixer, and not Durrell.

Eric could work cordially with any of his father's crew except Durrell. More nearly his age than any of the others, Durrell had been the bane of his existence for as long as he could remember. Because of his size, and that his older brother Dave was the job foreman, he could pretty well select tasks to suit himself.

They worked steadily for several minutes – both with trowels and taking turns spraying with the hose. Eric shifted the position of the mixer for Mike. Some of the tension began to wear off. Eric liked the diminutive "mud" carrier and they worked well together, synchronizing their motions, eliminating unnecessary talk and extra steps.

Carrying buckets of mud to his dad before lunch had been harder work, but now he shrank from any contact with Durrell or his father.

He glanced up from cleaning the mixer and saw Durrell approaching. Eric glanced around nervously.

"Well," Durrell sneered. "Paint any more of them purty pitchers, blondy?"

Eric ignored the fatigue in his shoulders and gave the mixer his focused attention.

Durrell persisted. "Wish I could take two hours for lunch. But then, I'm not the son of the boss – the panty-waisted baby boy."

Eric felt his throat tightening and knew his face was turning red, but he maneuvered his body until his back was to Durrell.

His antagonist sauntered closer. He laid a hand on Eric's shoulder. "Watch it, little blue eyes. Don't bruise your dainty hands! You might not be able to hold your crayons." He stuck his foot out to trip Eric and gave him a shove.

Eric was thrown back against the mixer. A burning pain crept along his neck and shoulder when he bounced against the steel drum. He spun around, bruised and angry. Dropping the hose, he lunged into the protruding belly of his assailant.

Durrell's enraged roar brought men running toward them. Eric felt hands pulling at him as he was separated from his tormentor.

In the embarrassing commotion that followed, he heard his dad's icy reprimand. "What in tarnation has gotten into you? Have you completely lost what little sense you ever had?"

"But, Dad," Eric sputtered.

"Just go home." He tossed him a quarter. "Call your mother to come get you."

***

Eric closed his eyes. Even the memory of it, after all these years, made him sick with shame. What an ass he had been that day! Yet, even now, he wished his father had been more understanding. He should have fired Durrell on the spot. But understanding was not one of his father's strong points.

Great Scott! Eric thought, *I'm 54 years old. Why would something that happened nearly forty years ago still bother me?* "Grow up, Eric," he said to the empty room.

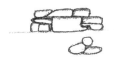

Chapter Five

ERIC WAS AWAKE before dawn. He lay in the bed he had slept in as a child and teenager and listened for sounds of his mother or Sherie in the kitchen. The house seemed lonely – but every place was lonely without Kate. "Sweetheart, I miss you!" he had told her last night when she picked up the phone. But, she sounded a little edgy when he kept pressing as to when she would join him at his family home.

"I don't know when I'm coming."

He tried not to show his disappointment. "Come when you can."

As soon as he heard a movement in the kitchen, he grabbed his robe and slipped down the stairs. Joel and Sherie's door was still closed, so it had to be his mother in the kitchen.

She looked up with a smile. "The coffee is ready. Do you remember where the cups are?"

"Good morning, Mom. Sure, I remember where the cups are, but I have to be very careful not to drink too much liquid."

Princess jumped up from her bed in the kitchen and stood in front of him, pleading with her brown eyes. He bent to pet her. When he didn't pick her up, she returned to her bed.

"She adjusted quickly, didn't she?" He sat down across the table from his mother and she started to get up to get his cup. "No, Mom, I'll get it. I just have to sit down a minute. Came down the stairs too fast."

She didn't make a point about his early fatigue. "I don't remember that you use to get up so early. Are you okay?"

38

"I don't always sleep well. I have pills but I hate to take them. I had a dream – not a pleasant one – last night." Using the table to lean on, he stood up. "I dreamed about the time I went to work and got in a fight with Durrell. Dad bawled me out in front of his whole crew, threw me a quarter and said to call you to come get me."

"I remember that you were not very happy." She offered him the sugar and cream.

"No thanks. I thought Dad would kill me when he got home."

"No, no," she fussed. "You don't mean that. Your dad never, ever, even whipped you."

He paused and sipped his coffee. "But, you didn't see how mad he was!"

"Well, he cooled off before he got home."

He poured them each another cup and declined her offer for breakfast. He wanted to wait to eat with the others. "Seems like it's working out for Joel and Sherie to be here with you."

She smiled. "Yes! It took so much of the burden off Betsy. I kept insisting I could stay alone. Then I took that stupid fall and broke my ankle. Of course, Sherie and Joel are gone a lot of the time. Little Princess will keep me company." At the sound of her name, the dog began plopping her tail. "Look how smart she is. Knows her new name already."

They sat quietly for a few minutes and neither felt the need for steady conversation. They simply enjoyed being together. Eventually, she broke the silence. "Did you expect your brother would become a national music star?"

"He practiced a lot. I used to kid him that his guitar sounded like two cats fighting. He has a beautiful voice."

"He used to slip off to practice at the quarry. Ed and Joel got into trouble going there, and you!" She shivered. "You decided to created a major tragedy there."

"No, Mom. Not me. Betsy was responsible for that terrible evening at the quarry. But, I did slip away to do some drawing there."

She stirred her coffee again. "I guess Kate stays busy with her writing."

"We both stay busy. I guess I ought to resign as Art Director, but in this electronic age of fax machines and e-mail, I can do most things at home. I go to the office about two days a week."

She finished her coffee. "That publishing company has been good for you."

"And I for them. I'm up for another Caldecott Award, Mom." He refilled her cup. "This is my fourth nomination."

"And do you think I'm surprised?"

He leaned down to kiss her forehead. "You and Grandma and Grandpa always believed in me." His voice was husky as it always was when he spoke of his grandfather. He refilled his cup and, picking up his cell phone, told his mother he was going for a short walk.

"But, it's dark." She followed him to the front porch and turned on the light.

"I'm not going far, Mom."

He walked cautiously after he left the circle of light provided by the porch light. Princess followed up to the edge of the circle and then turned to run back to the porch. It wasn't far to the granite wall that lined their yard on the side away from the B&B. He sat down on the wall slowly, careful not to spill his coffee. As he sipped from the cup, he rubbed the top of the wall. His wall. It stood for all that was bad – and good – in his childhood. He had lost count of the pictures Kate had taken of it on their trips to see his parents.

There was a wall between Kate and him now. He wished he could just take a bulldozer and knock it down.

His mother's sun-colored daffodils popped out in the early light like they were brushed with luminous paint. Already the busy hummingbirds were forging an early breakfast. They were the first birds on the scene each morning. Soon he heard the quiet chatter of the yellow goldfinches, who, except for black caps and black and

40

white wing feathers, could easily have been airborne daffodils. He listened to their short trills and the precise per- CHICK- a- tee calls.

If Kate came, she would be able to watch some of her favorite birds, the elegant rose-breasted-grosbeaks. Some years there were more of them than in other years, but they were gorgeous and wonderful subjects for paintings. He would ask his mom if she had seen any this spring – that might be an-

other incentive for his wife to join him.

He rubbed his unshaven jaw. Kate had become his wall of security for his adult years. He met her his first day at The Chicago Institute of Art. He had followed his dad's wishes and attended Appalachian State University in Boone for two years, taking every art course they offered. When he applied for and won the scholarship to the institute, he engaged in another battle with his father, but it was a less spirited quarrel than the others. He didn't want a partnership in his father's business and he left home on less than friendly terms.

After the first morning of orientation at the institute, he was assigned to a group of six and given a box lunch and an afternoon tour of the campus. Kate was working in the business office but served as a guide each orientation day. Eric couldn't help himself – he watched her all afternoon, marveling at her patience and admiring her knowledge of the institute and its objectives. She wore a white blouse, a long string of red beads and a flowing long red skirt that swirled sensually around her legs as she moved.

As they were closing down, he conjured enough nerve to approach her. "You took me to lunch. Let me take you to dinner."

Her eyes widened. He had been trying to figure out all morning if they were green or brown, but he suddenly realized they were a delightfully complex mix – a warm hazel. She was taller than most of the girls he knew; her brown hair reached the tip of his nose. She was slender and graceful as an ice skater, and she seemed completely unaware of her charm. He was studying her too intently, because it took a second for her answer to register.

"Lunch was a box lunch." She gave him a knee-weakening smile. "Are you going to take me to a hotdog stand?"

"We can go to a good Mexican restaurant – or, we can do Italian. There are so many cuisines in Chicago." He touched his back pocket and wondered how far his budget could stretch.

"There is a neat little Chinese restaurant at the corner of the apartment house where I live." She tilted her head up and he thought that it would be so easy to kiss her.

***

"Why are you an artist?" she asked as soon as they were seated. He mentioned love somewhere in his explanations, and she suddenly asked him for a definition of love. He told her he had never been in love and wondered if he could fall in love in one day.

Somewhere between the Wonton soup and the sushi, Eric realized exactly why God had led him to Chicago. And he told her.

"Don't be so hasty. I followed my Prince Charming to Chicago." She twisted her napkin.

His heart began sliding toward his stomach.

"Only, he turned out not to be so charming," confessed Katherine Anna Crenshaw, from the blue grass horse country of Lexington, Kentucky. Her eyes, until now, so full of fun, were focused on her hands.

His heart settled back into place.

As she reached up to brush a strand of hair back from her forehead, she said, "I hope you are not buttering me up so I'll pose as your model." She laughed and he was relieved to see little lines in the creases of her eyes relax.

Eric must have looked as confused as he felt.

"Surely, you understand that as a student at the Art Institute, you will have to hire a model."

"Oh, I don't want to paint *you*."

She hunched her shoulders and gazed at him. "Well, you are

brutally honest!"

"I want to be a better artist before I paint you, Kate."

Her cheeks turned pink and she looked at her plate. "I saw some of the paintings in your application portfolio. You are an excellent artist ... better than any of the other students."

"Do you really think so?" He hated it when his voice hiked in jubilation. He wanted to sound more sophisticated.

"You remind me of Andrew Wyeth, and sometimes you have a streak of Monet in you."

"Monet? If I remind you of Claude Monet, I'm better than I thought."

"Have you seen his *The Cliffs of Dieppe?*"

He snickered. "I've never been to Rome or Paris." He was surprised when she looked away, seemingly embarrassed by his attempt at a joke.

"What do you do on weekends?" he asked, searching for a way to end the awkward moment.

"Not much. What are you going to do?"

"First, I have to find a construction company that works on Saturday and get myself a job laying stone."

She reached across the table and touched his index finger, and he felt a tingle all though his body. "You're a stone mason? Isn't that dangerous for an artist."

"I've been doing it for years and my father and my grandfather before me. I'm not exactly an amateur."

"Please take care of your hands!" She laughed and reached for a fortune cookie.

"Believe me, I do," Eric said. "I might drop a stone on my foot, but not on my hands."

"I wish you could see the beautiful stonework on – well, the house I grew up in." Her smile faded, and a cloud moved across her eyes, as quickly as the evening fog from Lake Michigan.

"Your parents don't still live there?"

"My mother and brothers live there now, but – they may have to move." She grabbed her purse and sweater. Sensing her discomfort, he pried no more, but there was so much more he wanted to know about her.

She walked home rapidly and struggling to keep up, he acknowledged that the evening must have been a failure. "Hey, what did your fortune cookie say?"

Without breaking her rapid stride, she answered. "'Your date will be famous.' What did yours say?"

"Behave especially gentlemanly to girls with beautiful hazel eyes and long brown hair."

"Oh, you tease." She slowed her pace and he saw that the tight lines making a furrow in her forehead were gone.

He was delighted when at her door she asked him, "Would you consider going to the lake with me Sunday afternoon?"

"There is nothing in this world I would rather do!"

They spent every Sunday together after that. They found a small church to attend – at Kate's insistence – and spent afternoons hiking the beach and walking the boardwalk as she chewed on pink cotton candy. On inclement weather days, they visited art galleries. With her arm linked in his, her slender gloved hand encased in his, he ignored the wind whipping at their coats and the bone chilling dampness. He was accustomed to being a head taller than other men – but he had to contest the urge for a cavalier strut when she was on his arm. She was fun – wearing an array of ridiculous wool hats worn at jaunty angles. He exhausted adjectives for her hats – daffy, absurd, nutty, wacky.

He was a little intimidated to learn that she had visited many of the finest galleries in Europe with her father. She loved pointing out the work of the masters whose art she had seen in Paris or Rome.

"You should be lecturing at the Institute!" he said.

"No, I am much too shy and I really know very little."

"Oh, you are hardly shy!"

"Eric, there's a big difference between acting silly with a friend and lecturing to a room full of students!"

She knew a lot, and her innate perception of color and composition impressed him; he became a better artist because of her.

Friendly and mischievous, she had every security guard calling him Mr. Wyeth.

"Because," she said, "he's going to be just as good. My Chinese fortune cookie told me so." She knew the names of each uniformed officer but she made up nicknames for them: Inspector Clouseau from *The Pink Panther*, Hercule Poirot from Agatha Christie fame and *The Lone Ranger*. The guards loved her creativity.

Eric wondered why a beautiful, obviously educated woman was working at the art institute in a entry level position, but she shrugged off most of his questions. "I needed to do something different and I couldn't continue in graduate school. I love art and I need to help out with finances at home."

Kate often prepared a picnic lunch, but she never complained about the hot dogs and hamburgers he bought from the street vendors when he could afford it.

She seemed to enjoy his company but her cat hated him. "Why is your cat so afraid of me?" he asked her. As soon as Eric entered the apartment, the black cat, "Horseshoe" darted from the room. "I thought a horseshoe was supposed to bring good luck. Why doesn't she like me?"

"She doesn't like men, period. I think perhaps she was abused before I found her near the waterfront as a mangy half-dead kitten. I named her that because of the way she curls up to sleep reminding me of a horseshoe on our farm."

"You remind me of my sister, Bets. She keeps a whole menagerie of rescued animals."

"She sounds like my kind of a person."

He shared his family with her and spent several minutes describing the Blue Ridge Mountains. "Tell me about your farm," he invited.

Her father had owned a large horse farm and a string of racing horses. But his long fight with leukemia and eventual death had devastated the family – emotionally and financially. She didn't share the details until months later. He had seen the sorrow in her face when she spoke of her father, but, thinking of his experience, he assumed that the relationship had not been a good one. He worried and at first attributed her sadness to a continued interest in her Prince Charming – "who turned out not to be so charming."

One day as they walked along the boardwalk she asked him, "Have you ever watched someone you love die a slow, horrible death?" Her lips trembled.

"I watched my grandfather suffer. It nearly killed me when he died."

"It just about killed me when Dad died. I don't ever want to go through something like that again." She turned away from him and, when he touched her shoulder, he felt her trembling. Before either expected it, she was in his arms and he held her against his chest. As he kissed her, they heard a polite clapping from Rudolpho, with the Little Italy push cart. It intensified and grew into energetic applause as Eric released her. They bowed to the smiling street vendors and afternoon strollers on the boardwalk who were clapping.

"Bravo!" Rudolpho shouted. He pierced a fat pepperoni on a long fork and saluted them.

"I didn't mean to embarrass you, Kate."

She slipped her arm through his. "Dear Eric, I wasn't embarrassed. Were you?"

"Naw. I loved it."

The sun dropped low and Eric felt the evening chill. A heavy face-licking fog rolled in, like a mighty gray surf and he wanted to get her out of the weather. He couldn't stand the thought of her catching a cold.

He steered her toward their bus stop.

They walked in silent communion, and he told himself there was no need for talk.

A burly man jostled them in the fog and murmured his apology. He had knocked her hat askew.

Eric stepped in front of her and, using both hands, tried to reposition the little cloth hat.

She took hold of his wrists. "It's all right. Thank you for another glorious day."

He bent to kiss her, but she delayed him with a finger at his lips. "Wait, Eric. To me, this is no simple crush. I love you," she whispered.

He drew his head back. "And I love you – you know."

"I didn't know."

He crushed her to him. Surely, she must have known. He gave her a passionate kiss. There was no clapping this time – but it seemed to him that the angels were singing. It was a holy moment for him and he wanted to praise God, to thank Him. He raised his right arm as though he was directing the celestial choir in Handel's magnificent *Messiah*. Hal-le-lu-jah.

He sustained the last phrase, voicing it aloud. "Hal-lee-luu-jah." He brought his hand down to his side.

"Hal-le-lu-jah," she whispered, and her eyes were shining with tears.

"Darling," Eric said as they neared her apartment, "your dad must have been a wonderful man and I am so sorry."

"You remind me of my dad – gentle, kind and smart."

"I don't know about the rest of it, but I am smart enough to know I want to spend the rest of my life with you."

***

Eric saw other lights going on in the house. He was to be ready for Bets by eight so he had to hurry. He had intended to call Kate again, but it was still too early at her folks' house in western Kentucky.

The clinic had his faxed records and with only a few preliminaries, he was able to check in. He began the series of blood pressure checks – taken while he was standing and then while he was sitting. In the last few months he had become more aware of his blood pressure than his bank account. After weighing in, he was escorted to the treatment room. A lounge chair, similar to the one he used in New York, made him feel comfortable. There were about ten chairs on either side of the room, separated from each other by compact hemodialyzers. All the blood in his body would circulate through that machine in the next four hours and the toxins filtered out.

The arrangement was not conducive to conversation between the patients and added to a sense of isolation. No food or drinks, or company – it was enough to call for a "pity party," but Eric wasn't given to self pity. He enjoyed a fine career, and he had a wonderful marriage, until recently. He couldn't complain. He just didn't want his life, or his marriage, to end! Especially his marriage. He wanted it the way it used to be.

After the nurse on duty had him connected, he leaned back to listen to the quiet hum of the machine that would become his kidneys. He hadn't realized he was so worn out, and he couldn't focus on reading, so he relaxed, sometimes sleeping and sometimes daydreaming about that eventful night his father came home after firing him from the job.

***

Not a word did his father say to him during supper.

Eric had heard his truck come into the back yard at dusk. He listened to his father unloading his tools and washing up in the laundry room. He came quietly to the table and the others entered the dining room and found their places.

Eric scrutinized the long, thin face, but he saw no clue to indicate what his father was thinking. He asked the blessing in his normal, quiet voice, ending with his usual, "Make us your servants. Amen." He reached for the platter and then passed the meatloaf to Eric.

Eric had trouble swallowing. Food stuck in his throat like stale peanut butter. He felt a terrible sense of apprehension. When was the ax going to fall across his neck? He paid no attention to Betsy's continuous patter about her animals. Eric found her high-pitched voice more irritating than usual.

It seemed like the longest supper on record, but eventually, his father stood up and as though nothing was unusual, he thanked his wife for the fine meal.

"Come with me," he said to Eric, and Eric nearly knocked his chair over getting up. His legs were wobbly and moved woodenly as he complied. They went through the house and across the front porch with his dog Soccer following. They crossed the wide lawn in the waning light and still his father didn't speak.

Was it a whipping he was planning?

Mr. Walsh stepped across a narrow stream and strode to the edge of the graveled shoulder of the road.

Was he going to tell his son to hit the road, leave home by

taking the road right back into town? Maybe there were other incidents, similar to this, that explained why Eric's two older brothers had left home so young.

Finally, his father stopped. In the gathering dusk, Eric was unable to read his facial expressions, except for the stern jut of his jaw. His uneasiness turned to consternation when his father said simply, "You cannot work with me."

Eric's throat was collapsing in on itself. Certainly he had disappointed his father but were a few hours of missed work grounds for total disgrace? His dad looked at him, but Eric avoided eye contact.

"I'll let you work alone. Right here. By yourself. You can learn a craft or you can dawdle away your time as you choose – but no one else will be dependent on you. I'll hold you responsible for the work, but I'll not hang around to nag you."

Eric choked on a bubble of air that rose and fell in his throat. He was confused about what his father was saying. The quiet, deliberate voice droned on.

"If you want to devote your life to painting pictures, that's your choice, but I just believe you'll need some trade to support yourself."

Mr. Walsh leaned over and patted a small mound of rocks that Eric hadn't noticed before. "There used to be a stone wall here. I've been meaning to replace it ever since we bought the land. You will gather the stones and rebuild the wall this summer."

Eric stared at the pile of stones.

His father began speaking again, quietly and it was as though he was speaking to himself. "God knows I'm not any great shakes as a father. But, by hokey," he grew emphatic, "while you are living at home, you are going to have to work." He hesitated. "I'll leave the scale up to you. I expect you to do some research. You might check that stone wall down by the church that borders the cemetery. Also, your gram can find you some drawings and notes of your grandpa's." He pointed up the hill

49

to the old apple tree at the back of their property line. "It should follow the ridge and extend it to that tree."

Eric could hardly make out the tree in the gathering darkness. His father looked at him for a long time, and Eric tried to keep from squirming under the stare.

"Can you handle that?"

Eric gulped. His voice sounded strange. "I think so. I hope so. I'll try."

Mr. Walsh turned and took a few steps toward the house where someone had turned the porch lights on. He stopped and faced Eric again. "The first rule my dad taught me: lay one stone on two, and two stones on one. And Eric, find yourself a good pair of gloves." He started off again, paused and his voice sounded sad. "Son, I know Durrell wasn't nice to you. Mike told me. Durrell isn't nice to a lot of people – he has big time trouble at home – but he desperately needs the job and frankly, I need him just as much as he needs me. You'll be going back to school. I put him on probation."

But you bawled me out in front of the whole crew. You humiliated me and didn't say a thing to Durrell when everybody could hear you. He wished he could tell his dad that he was sorry about disappointing him.

Eric sat down on what was left of the old wall. Soccer came to him and leaned his head against his leg. Eric put his arms around the little dog. He was stung by his father's decision not to let him work with him, but he had gotten off pretty easy. He could work at his own speed and on his own time. Then, he smarted. *Probation?* Better that than a prisoner sentenced to hard labor on the rock pile. He rubbed his neck. "One on two. Two on one."

The only good news was that he didn't have to be around Durrell – or his father.

Suddenly, the summer stretched out ahead of him – beautiful and exciting! What were a few hours of work on a stone wall? It might be a little tiring to gather enough stones, but the woods were full of them. His mother complained that her garden sprouted rocks. They called their place "Walsh's Stone Mountain."

How high did the wall have to be? Well, from the few rocks

still standing from the old wall, it wouldn't have to be more that a couple of feet. "Big deal," he said aloud to Soccer.

Tomorrow he would take a jaunt on his bicycle to the church and take a few measurements of that wall. Maybe he would lay a few yards of stone after lunch.

Chapter Six

Eric reached Kate in the evening. "Sweetheart," he said, "if you don't come soon, the vacation will be gone and you won't spend any time with my family."

She was silent for a moment and he wanted desperately to see her – to touch her and to pull her into his arms.

"Eric, I remember that you didn't stop by to see my family on your flight to North Carolina."

"Oh, honey, I'm sorry. It's just that the clinic–"

"They have dialysis clinics in Kentucky."

"I don't know what to say."

***

He hadn't known what to say a few years ago when he hurt her so much either. He was commuting from their home in Westchester County to the city each day. She had planned to work on her graduate degree after their marriage but, after the birth of their children, she was content to stay at home and care for them.

One evening she handed him a large envelope and asked him to give it to Ellie, the Juvenile Fiction Editor at the Greenbrier Publishing Company where he worked.

"Ellie is expecting it." She glowed with excitement.

"May I look?"

"I hoped you would want to."

He opened the envelope and pulled out about thirty pages of a manuscript. He read the first page and perused the rest. "This is good. Why did you ... When?" he stammered.

"I guess I have the empty nest syndrome, with Kathy and Clay gone."

It was a children's book about a young boy going fishing and accidently getting his hook caught in his worst enemy's baseball cap. It was based on the first time Eric took Clay fishing. On his first

cast, Clay snagged his hook in his dad's cap. By changing the characters, Kate's hero conquered the town's bully. Eric laughed out loud at some of the dialogue in Kate's manuscript.

But, he didn't give it to Ellie the next day, and the day after she took a short trip. A week later he delivered it to the editor. He hurried home, eager tell Kate that they both had an appointment the next day with the editorial department.

He placed a large artist's portfolio on the table.

"Both of us?" she asked, staring at the portfolio. She leaned over and cautiously opened it up. "Oh," she said. "The illustrations are beautiful."

Then, she turned and left the room.

He stared speechlessly after her.

He found her in the rose garden. He tried to put his arms around her but she moved away.

"What have I done wrong? Don't you like the sketches? They will be better in color."

She wouldn't look at him but she said quietly, "Didn't you think my work was good enough to stand on its own?"

He understood then and was sick at heart. He lifted her face and held it with both hands when she tried to back away. "I knew your work was great. I didn't want Ellie to assign it to another artist."

"But you said you didn't want to illustrate books!"

"But that was before I saw your book. I am so sorry, darling. I'll talk to Ellie the first thing in the morning."

She reached up to take his hands down and slid into his arms. "I don't want anyone but you to illustrate my book – I just wanted to have it accepted first, so I would know it stood on its own."

The next year the joke was on him because she won the prestigious Newbery Award for the year's best written children's book. It took him two more years to win the Caldecott Award, the highest award for illustrating children's books.

He undressed and put on his robe, tied it and looked around the room. It wasn't much like it had been when he lived at home. Grandchildren had stayed in it many times and not many of his belongings were still here, except the furniture.

He walked to his old desk and opened the top drawer – only pencils and some stationery. He went through the drawers on the left side and was getting discouraged by the time he opened the last drawer on the right. He pulled out a folder and went to the bed and propped up his pillows before he got in. He remembered his reaction of surprise when he saw the drawings for the first time.

They were fine line drawings, delicate and yet intricately executed in black ink. He stared at the pictures of blacksmith forges, lumber kilns, stone bridges, walls and numerous chimneys. They illustrated various steps of work, and Eric was fascinated the first night he studied his grandfather's drawings and notes. He remained fascinated, all these years later, at the sketches of many of the jobs the father and son team had completed together.

The drawings were exquisite, with a touch of the whimsy. Beside one wall Eric discovered a lovely rendition of a tiger lily, complete with mouth and whiskers. Tucked into a fireplace, a tiny field mouse grinned at him.

He was struck by the beauty in the symmetry of design and pleasing lines and for the first time he saw the art in his father's craft. Under some of the drawings his grandpa had penciled in, "Easy on the eyes." Eric recognized the saying. It was also his father's way of signifying a particularly successful endeavor – reserved only for the best.

He thumbed through other pages tonight, just as he had that

year when he was fifteen. He found an interesting discussion of early mixtures for chinking fireplaces. He read about "mud and stick" chimneys in which the mud baked to a hard pottery.

There was a warning about bees digging holes in mud chinking and a drawing of a comical little man being chased from a chimney riddled with bees. The bees gave a hardy pursuit. Kate had to see this, Eric thought. She would come up with a good book manuscript.

He reviewed a list of rules and noted the classic proportions for a wall: two feet rising from a three foot base. He nodded gravely. The construction of the church wall conformed nicely.

There was a description of the hidden joint technique, where only the thinnest layer of mortar was used and the chimney appeared to be laid mortarless, like his dry wall.

His grandfather told about massive stairs he had crafted from stone. "Started with a five hundred pound block of sandstone and by the end of the day, I'd whittled it down to size – to about a hundred and fifty pounds. Chip by chip. This went on for six days."

In discussing why a fireplace must "draw" properly, his grandfather described one that didn't. "When a puff of wind would come up, the whole house would fill with smoke and children would run from it hollering and crying."

Just as he had as a lad, Eric went to sleep with the papers on the bed beside him.

***

Eric slept late the next morning. The family had already eaten. He didn't care. Eating had become a chore to him, but Kate kept prodding him along. Apparently she had sent instructions to his mother, because she insisted that he eat his vitamins and proteins.

He wandered out the back door to the porch. His mother was busy in her herb garden, with Princess beside her. Eric started to join her, but he was arrested by the music coming from the studio. Sherie was singing, with Joel strumming his guitar. Her voice was clear and melodic. Joel joined her, his deeper voice blending in beautiful harmony and adding a deeper tone to the music. That's the way marriage should work, Eric noted.

Kate preferred opera and the "long hair" music but she would have to admit today that nothing could be more enchanting and soothing than the duet that reached him now. He had grown up with the mournful Appalachian music and less formal country with the fiddle and the guitar and the banjo.

He started down the steps to go to the studio but didn't want to interrupt their work. His mother had seen him and was hurrying toward him followed by the dog.

"Just let me get a cup of coffee," he insisted in the kitchen.

"And disobey Kate. Not on your life," his mother said, pulling out pans.

"Nobody disobeys Kate," he muttered gruffly, and hoped his mother had not heard him.

But, she had. When she placed a plate of eggs and toast in front of him, Princess reared up on her hind legs to beg.

"No, you don't, you little beggar, Mom fixed this for me!"

His mom picked the dog up and petted her. "Why do I have the feeling that things are not as they should be between you and Kate?"

He struggled with his emotions, bowing his head and rubbing his forehead. He knew he had not fooled his mother, so he confided. "There's a wall between us. We disagree about the possibility of a kidney transplant."

His mom gasped. "Transplant? What on earth are you talking about, Eric?"

"I didn't want to tell you over the telephone. I wanted to be here to tell you that my kidneys are failing and there is nothing else to do. I have to have a transplant. It's okay, Mom."

He moved around to put his arm around her. "I'm registered on the City Hospital's list for a transplant, Mom, but Kate is afraid I won't get one in time. I have a difficult blood type to match. People with type O negative can only accept an organ from a donor with type O negative blood." He studied her blue eyes. Did she understand what he was saying? "Of course, I took a chance when we started this vacation because if a match became available while we are away, I couldn't get home in time." Then, seeing alarm in her face, he added, "It's unlikely I could get one this soon, anyway."

"Is there an alternative?" His mother was awesome. "You hinted, from the tone of your voice, that there might be an alternative."

"Mom, I will gladly accept at kidney from a brain-dead donor. But I can't feel right about taking one from someone who is alive and has years ahead of him – even if it is a perfect match."

"Have you found such a match.?"

"Yes, Clay. My *son* wants to be the donor. My twenty-eight year old son! I can't do it, Mom."

"Oh," so very quietly that he almost didn't hear it. "Yes, I can see that would present a dilemma. That's what Kate was talking about. Let me think about that for awhile."

Eric jerked his chin up. "What do you mean – 'what Kate meant'?"

His mom stood up to clear the plates from the table. "She told me that – well, I just didn't understand." She sat back down to be on eye level with him. "She told me that you were having a serious problem thinking things through. She is so worried, son!" She reached across to touch his hand. "You two have had almost a story-book romance and she can't stand the idea of your not agreeing on something so important. Is she concerned about Clay?"

"Yeah, and I am. too. There is a remote possibility, but a possibility – never the less – that Clay could become a casualty. At least one person has lost his life after donating a kidney."

"No, that's not what she meant." His mom wrinkled her brow and tapped her cheek, a mannerism he remembered so well as a kid. She was having trouble expressing herself. "Kate told me that Clay had a passion for something you would not accept. I wondered if he had been drawn to one of those strange new religions."

Eric laughed. He hadn't realized Kate had been talking to his mother so much. They each retreated into their own thoughts, then his mom voiced the very horror he was contemplating. "Could Clay inherit the kidney disease?"

"That was our first thoughts – since Grandpa died of kidney failure. He, however, had severe diabetes, and his problem was complicated by that. My kidney failure is due to some injury. It could be some of those horrific accidents I had on the ski slopes, trying to learn to ski, or even that car wreck I was in soon after we moved to New York. The doctors do not think Clay is in danger – but they can't know for sure. That's why I can't be comfortable with the donation of one of his kidneys."

"Of course you would be concerned." She patted his hand. "We need to pray about it."

They sipped their coffee before his mother began quietly, "Eric. if your daughter, Kathy needed a kidney, would you allow Clay to donate one to her?"

Eric put his cup down on the table. He couldn't answer her. Of course he would not allow Kathy to die. Mom accepted his silence, but she startled him. "Perhaps Kate cannot see the difference."

Eric fought an urge to get up and walk out of the kitchen. His mother continued talking. "Clay was such an unusual boy. When he and Kathy came to spend their summers with us, Kathy would spend every minute she could with Betsy. Clay followed your father around like a puppy."

Eric chuckled. "Dad gave him his own set of tools." Eric pushed his cup around on the table. "Did I ever tell you about the time I lost Clay in the Yankee Stadium? You remember what a sports fan he has always been. We made several trips to the stadium. We called it our 'Boy's Night Out,' – and we still do it occasionally. I believe that it was the first time we went there. Clay went to the restroom just before everyone started to exit. After a little while, I got anxious because the crowd was thinning out, and I couldn't find my son. I finally alerted security and I was getting panicky. Then, something made me go back to where we had been sitting to watch the game.

"There sat Clay, serenely watching everybody leave. He looked up at me and asked, 'Did you know that there is a little boy lost in the stadium? I heard it over the loud speaker. I wonder why his dad didn't teach him like you taught me? You told me that if I ever got lost while we were camping to just sit down and wait.'

"I didn't care how macho Clay thought he was," Eric continued, "I just had to take him in my arms to hug him."

Mom laughed quietly. "Albert's biggest disappointment was

that the two of them didn't get to finish their project together."

"Project?"

"You know, the outdoor grill over near Joel's studio."

"I didn't know. I'll have to look at it." He began to laugh, almost to himself. "You know what? Dad wanted me to be a stone mason. I became an artist, more or less. I wanted Clay to become a lawyer – you have to admit, he has the brains, and the ability to argue – especially the ability to argue – to become a lawyer. He became a stone mason!"

The back screen door opened and Sherie and Joel came in.

"We thought you were going to sleep all day," Sherie said.

"Speaking of sleeping, I found the hammock." Joel said. "We'll put it up out in the yard and you can take your afternoon rests out there."

"Only if you and Sherie will promise to sing. That music this morning was beautiful. Are you working on another CD?'

"We are *always* working on another CD. Joel never rests. Eric, do you think Kate would mind if I called again to urge her to come?"

"I don't know. I can't seem to get through to her."

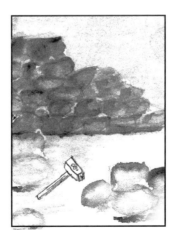

Chapter Seven

Soon after lunch, Eric invited Princess to go with him to the hammock. He lifted her to his chest and as he rubbed her ears, she curled up for her afternoon nap. *Someday*, Eric thought, letting his mind race, *when I least expect it, I'm going to get the call that will save my life. Oh, the audacity of these thoughts! For one to receive an organ – most likely – another had to die. I don't wish that, God.*

Failing health was an severe jolt to Eric. An avid hiker and outdoors man, he played squash three times a week at his health club. He donated blood at City Hospital as often as they'd let him before he got sick. He considered it a responsibility because of his O negative blood type. He wasn't bitter, but the tough change in his life was disconcerting. His hiking and fishing trips with Clay were over, apparently.

His parents had a hammock similar to this one and hanging from this same tree when he and Kate brought the children to visit his parents the summer Clay was ten. As they began packing to leave, his father said to his mother, "Sybil, let's ask Kate and Eric to let us keep the kids here for the rest of the summer! What fun would they have in a city apartment building?"

The kids were ecstatic, so they went to Boone and bought a couple more pairs of blue jeans and shorts for each of them. Kathy got a little homesick that first year, but Clay was in all his glory. The children continued their annual two months summer visits until Clay was thirteen. By then, they had moved to the suburbs and Eric's father's health was beginning to fail. Clay was involved in sports and didn't want to leave his friends.

Clay had made good grades in high school. But college? Since he knew exactly what he wanted to do with his life, going to college seemed like a waste of time and money to him.

"Just give me a chance to do what I want to do. Okay, Dad?"

Remembering his quarrels with *his* father, Eric agreed. Three years later, after working with some of the top contractors in the area, Clay opened up his own business as a stone mason, and became a sought-after craftsman. A year later, he married Eric's favorite secretary, Jane. It was a good deal for all of them because Jane continued to work for Eric in his home office and also worked as Clay's secretary and bookkeeper.

Eric reminisced. Had his father really mellowed by the time Clay was a boy or did he just understand him better? He seemed to have far more patience with his grandchildren. Eric went to sleep dreaming about the summer he was fifteen.

***

Riding his bicycle down the mountain, Eric felt again a glorious sense of jubilation. If he had been a musician, like Joel, instead of a budding artist, he would have burst forth into song. The mountains and valleys were flooded with morning sunshine and yellow dandelions made a neon border along the road.

His neck was stiff and sore where he had hit the concrete mixer, but that was a small price to pay for the freedom he felt today. He planned to take advantage of the brilliant sunshine.

He figured he'd have to dally around on the wall a little just to let his dad know he'd been working. He would draw a string first, straight up the hillside to the old apple tree, and he would pile a few rocks to give the impression he'd begun the endeavor. But as he peddled toward the church, his mind was on the art work he planned to display at the Summer Art Festival in Banner Elk.

When he got to the church, he propped his bike against a hickory tree and walked over to the wall. Not much to that structure! He was impressed, however, with the massiveness of the wall, even though it didn't have much height.

He took out his steel tape and began some measurements. Almost three feet wide at the base, narrowing to two feet at the top. This wall seemed to stretch for blocks. Strange, he said to himself. He had never noticed the symmetry of the dimensions. The gray stones contrasted nicely with the green foliage. In the winter they would be the same color as the nearby woods.

Eric heard a lawnmower and turned to see the caretaker of the church coming around the back of the building. He watched with interest as the old man turned off the machine and strode over to him. He recognized that it was Pastor Earl, the retired minister. All he needed was to don a red suit to become Santa Claus. He was the patriarch of Mountain View Church. For many years, when the church couldn't afford to pay a pastor, he held it together with his folksy preaching. Long retired as a high school teacher, he still maintained the grounds and kept the young pastor in line.

"Admiring the wall?" he asked.

"Yes, sir. I'm going to build one like it."

"One like it? " He studied Eric over the rim of his glasses. "Good luck." He pulled on his beard. "You are one of the Walsh boys, I believe. The youngest of the boys? I haven't talked to you in a long time."

"Yes, sir. I'm Eric."

"Don't look much like the other two." Eric felt a wave of annoyance as the old man looked him over. "I wasn't expecting the yellow hair. I guess you look like your mom, and the others take after your dad."

Eric leaned over to run his hand along the cool side of the wall. "Got skin on it, doesn't it?"

Eric jerked his hand up. "I beg your pardon?"

"An old Irish friend of mine used that word to describe a smooth wall. But around here we just say it has a 'slick face.'"

Eric nodded. "It certainly doesn't have any gaps or rugged edges. I don't see any mortar."

"Oh, mortar just takes the interest out of a wall. Make it too uniform and you might just as well pour a concrete wall. It would be most unsatisfying. The reason the old walls were built without mortar was so they could adjust to winter without freeze heaving."

Eric thought that it made good sense. He was relived he would be spared the time and effort of mixing mortar.

"Man like me – old as the hills – knows a good wall when he see it. This one was built for permanence."

"What do you mean – permanence?" What would you expect from stone, for crying out loud.

"I have seen a few stone walls that didn't last more than a dozen years. The foundation on this one was built to last a century or two."

"Foundation?" Eric felt a slight trepidation and a little quiver of apprehension.

Pastor Earl was warming to his subject, but Eric was getting impatient, and he hoped he would be spared a lengthy sermon. "Good wall is like a good life – has to have a good foundation."

"What kind of a foundation? For a wall, I mean."

"Below the frost line, of course. Maybe twelve inches here. Higher up, eighteen inches."

Eric felt a growing sense of foreboding and not quite so confident. "Do you mean that if I build a wall like this, I have to dig a trench and pour a foundation a foot below ground level?"

"If you build a wall like this one. Of course," he paused. Then in a more friendly voice he said, "The old timers used rocks they placed below ground as their foundation. So if you build one like this one, use rocks for your foundation."

Eric studied the wall and was quizzical. "It is much broader at the base," he said quietly.

"Broad-based bottom. Adds stability." Pastor Earl put his hand on his white beard and brushed it, stoking it, pulling it out to a point below his chin. "Why don't you discuss it with your dad? He can tell you anything there is to know about a stone wall."

Eric rubbed his neck. It has begun to hurt in direct proportions to the realization of the enormity of the project and the startling surprise about the shovel work he was going to be forced to do this summer. "Thanks, but I want to surprise my dad. Sir, what is the purpose of a wall like this?"

"These walls enhance the landscape and define boundaries. Did you ever read Robert Frost's poem, 'Mending Fences'?"

"Uh, uh."

"The poet said the 'Good fences make good neighbors'."

"Oh."

"I think Joshua might have had a little more trouble had the walls around Jericho been built like this one."

"Oh." Eric was not feeling especially intelligent.

Brother Earl cocked his head and smiled. "I' m sure you re-member the account in the Bible when God's man made the walls tumble down as his men marched around the town, shouting and blowing trumpets. There is a wonderful Negro spiritual, "Joshua Fought the Battle of Jericho'."

"Yes." Eric said. "I think I remember that song."

"Well, good luck, son. Care if I come by to observe the work once in awhile?"

Suddenly, Eric had a lot less self confidence. "I have the feeling that I'm going to need all the advice I can get." He must have upset his father far more than he had realized. His summer was going to be consumed by hard, gray rocks. The afternoon sketching trip to the quarry he had planned was out of the question.

Anger scalded his throat. He kicked pebbles out of his way as he returned to his bicycle. What was it with his dad? He was hardly the prodigal son. He had spent his whole life trying to win his dad's approval and for effort, he had been condemned to the rock pile like a criminal.

He yanked his bike toward him and with his foot, booted the kick-stand up. He visualized the whole dreary summer looming ahead – one gigantic collection of boulders. Eric of the chain gang. He threw his leg over the bike and headed home. Slowly.

Chapter Eight

After he had talked with Kate that evening, he dialed Clay, but his line was busy. Eric lay in the bed thinking of his son. They had named him in honor of Kate's father and to Kate's delight he was developing a personality much like his grandfather – easygoing, hard working and full of fun. When Clay was about three, he found his dad napping one Sunday afternoon. He climbed up onto Eric's chest and pried open one of Eric's eyelids.

"Dad," he asked, "are you still in there?"

Eric gabbed his son in a bear hug and covered him with kisses. "I'm here and I'm going to eat you up!" he growled.

Eric could almost hear the squeals of laughter. Tonight, he felt a lump in his throat. How he loved that boy who had grown into a man and who wanted to risk his life to save his dad!

He dialed Clay again.

"What's up, Dad? Anything wrong?" He sounded worried.

"Why do you always ask that when I call?"

"You don't call often."

The comment irritated Eric, partly because he knew it was true. He stood up and shuffled around the room. The next question would be about his health so he quickly asked, "Remember the outside fireplace and barbeque you and your grandfather were building?"

Clay sounded so *young*, hardly twenty eight. "Of course I do. Grandpa taught me everything I know about stone masonry. But we never got to finish it, unless he did later."

Eric rubbed his jaw. He glanced at the mirror, suddenly felt very *old*. He moved so he could look out the window. "Would you care if I finished it?"

"Are you sure that you are able to?"

"Look, kid, I'm certainly not the mason you are now, but I suspect I'm as good as you were at thirteen." He hoped his voice didn't sound irritated .

"Dad, I mean are you physically able to do it? I wasn't knocking your skills."

Eric wanted to remind his son that he had worked his way through college laying stone, first in Boone and later in Chicago. Clay would just remind him that he had heard the story hundreds of times. "I guess the only way we'll know is for me to try it."

"Just don't work too hard. Boy, I wish I could come down to help! I miss the mountains, and you and Mom, so much. Are you visiting any of your old friends?"

Eric had often told him about his boyhood buddy, Merwyn. After the call, he lay in bed, wide awake for a long time. Was he able? He would check the tool shed early, before he left for the clinic. He could stop by the building supply store after his dialysis.

Eventually, he slept and he dreamed about Merwyn.

***

The hours after Eric spoke with Pastor Earl were discouraging. His melancholy was not lessened by the hard work. His dad had left an old, rusty steel wheelbarrow, with a bent front wheel, making it hard to push. Eric followed the faint trace of an old logging road, gathering stones and dumping them into the wheelbarrow.

A gray squirrel resented his intrusion. Leaping from limb to limb in the tall oak tree, his bushy tail balancing his flight like a rudder, he screamed his contempt.

"Go away!" Eric yelled. "I have enough misery without your sass."

His shoulders ached, his back throbbed and his winter-softened hands were already blistering. The weight of the stones increased dramatically as the day wore on. They became more and more unwieldy and demonstrated not one ounce of cooperation. Unstable, they were hard to stack properly and often rolled down the hill onto the road. He was forever being delayed in order to tote a few back up on the hill to be balanced again on top of his pile. He grew weary of wrestling with them and was disgusted with his own clumsiness.

He had his back to the road, intent on his work, and he didn't notice the bicycle approaching. Now his spine stiffened as he heard the squeaky voice of Merwyn McNeil. That was all he needed.

"What'cha doing?"

Eric sighed, slowly straightened his back and faced his long-time crony. "What does it look like I'm doing? Playing Chinese checkers?"

"You're too close to the road to be building a fort."

Eric had the urge to pick up a hefty stone and hurl it at Merwyn. "If you can't figure out what I'm doing, I haven't got time to explain."

"I thought you were going to work for your dad this summer. Get fired already?" His laugh grew to a nerve-wracking cackle that billowed into Eric's face like a puff of poisoned smog.

Eric sputtered, "Go home, Wyn. I'm working." His neck and ears turned warm.

Merwyn smirked. "You getting paid for doing this?"

Eric blew dust from his gloves. Perhaps if he ignored his tormentor, he'd go away.

Merwyn laid his bike down and scrambled onto the rock pile, dislodging a couple of them that began to roll, throwing him off balance. He let out a yelp and dropped to all fours, narrowly averting a landslide, but ripping the knee of his jeans.

For the first time in days, Eric laughed. "You mess up my pile or get blood on the rocks, and I'll have your hide."

Merwyn pulled at the tear. "My mom will have my hide."

Eric ignored him.

"I *assume* you're *attempting* to build something. A stone fence, probably. I guess you know you have to dig a foundation."

"How come you know so much about building a stone wall?"

Wyn looked hurt. "How come? Man, I'm an expert on walls. But you need bricks."

"Bricks? How am I going to get bricks?"

"I think the Chinese cut them out of a mountain. I read an article in *The National Geographic* about the Great Wall of China. Do it that way and you won't need so many rocks." Wyn moved closer. He stretched his arm out toward the outline on the ground that Eric had marked off with lime. "You need some help."

"Go home, Wyn." Eric's voice quivered with aggravation.

"Also, if you fill the middle with rammed earth and sticks, you won't need so many rocks. See, we can just tamp the dirt down and it gets hard –" He reached for the shovel.

"No, you don't. And there is no 'we' to this job." They engaged in a tug of war over the shovel.

Eric shouted, "Get away or I'll bury you with this shovel."

Wyn let go of the shovel and Eric fell backwards. Wyn straightened his shoulders and brushed his hands together. "Have it your way, but you're missing a great chance. That wall I read about is over 4,000 miles long and has lasted for centuries."

They glared at each other, then Wyn shrugged his shoulders. "I'm going for a cool, refreshing swim in the quarry. Wanna go?"

"I've got work to do. Can't play all summer like some pampered kid I know. Anyway, it's illegal to swim in the quarry."

"So? Didn't stop you last week."

"So?" Eric mimicked. "Go home. I'm working."

Merwyn walked to his bike. "I think I might just fall in love this summer. Have you seen the new girls who moved to town?"

"Love!" Eric scoffed. "You haven't hit puberty."

***

The next morning, Eric checked the tool shed before he left for town. His father had carefully cleaned his tools and put them in his tool box. Eric felt a lump in his throat. His dad's tool shed was almost holy ground. A wave of sadness washed over him. Kate still grieved for her father also.

He picked up a heavy stone hammer and a smaller one that was used
to chip off corners so a rock would fit.
He held his father's chisel in his hand
and imagined his father using it, split-
ting stones, cutting them to fit. He
picked up an eight inch long pitching
tool. He could see his father shearing off a hump on a stone. With a
sense of reverence, he put everything back. He would have to stop by
the building supply on his way home from dialysis.

Chapter Nine

On the way to the clinic, Eric drove slowly to enjoy the scenery. Just beyond the home place, a deer vaulted across the road in two leaps. "Deja vu," he said aloud.

About half way to Linville he pulled to the side of the road at his favorite spot where the trees drew back from the sides of the road, like theater curtains, to reveal a dramatic vista. The rugged peak of Grandfather Mountain was awesome, piercing the clouds, gray boulders stark against the pink-tinged clouds. Standing beside the car, he had to lift his chin, head tilted back to study the summit. The view from Foscoe showed the face of Grandfather, and he would watch it from that angle on his ride back from Boone. The mountain spoke to him today. The granite represented the enduring stability of his life; the wisps of clouds reflected the capricious uncertainties he faced. He desperately needed answers.

This whole contemplation was absurd because a week ago he knew exactly what he was going to do – rather, what he was *not* going to do.

He climbed into the car to drive to the clinic, gripping the steering wheel. His thoughts lingered on the mountain. When he next painted the scene he must let Grandfather Mountain dominate the canvas, revealing the grandeur. "Majestic," he whispered.

He found himself being caught up with the visual drama in the quiet, early morning, tensions relaxing. Was he imaging things? He could hear a church choir singing, "Majesty, worship His majesty ... "

It hadn't occurred to him, in a long time, to give credit to the

Deity. Mom had said, "We must pray about this."

Pray? He had not prayed – really prayed – in years.

Perhaps it was his illness that was making this an issue.

***

They took him right away at the clinic. A cheerful nurse, Lou Ann, from her name tag, picked up his chart. "Good morning, Mr. Walsh. Step on the scales first and then let's check your blood pressure."

Walking with him to his station, she said, "We need some pictures for these walls."

"Yes, you certainly do."

Her response was not one he expected. "Maybe you could contribute one. I'm a big fan of yours, especially after I saw one of your shows in Abington, Virginia a few years ago. Actually, you won't remember, I was in an art class with you at ASU."

He was surprised. "Do you paint?"

"No. I tried – once. I demonstrated as much talent as a boiled egg."

"Who said so?"

"Professor McCluskey."

Eric could only chuckle. He remembered Professor McCluskey. Lou Ann had better stick to nursing.

He followed her down the hall, wondering how he could have forgotten her long, red hair. Of course, she might not have been a redhead in school.

She continued, "I'm also friends with Sherie and Joel."

"Oh, do you sing?"

"No, not me." She laughed. "But I can cook up a scrumptious bowl of chicken and dumplings."

"Ah! The important things. I'll bet your chicken and dumplings are low in sodium – and all those evil spices that make food worth eating! I'll paint a special scene for the clinic." He almost added, "If I live long enough," but she might take it as an evaluation of her work.

While she was connecting the fistula to the machine, and taking his blood pressure again, she confessed, "I keep up with the rich and the famous. I own a couple of your prints – small ones."

Eric considered telling her about Kate lugging his paintings to galleries all over Chicago and New York City. Kate – with her passion for his work. Kate, with her absolute faith that he would be greatly reverend for his art. Kate, who didn't want to watch him die.

Lou Ann was busy, moving on to the next patient.

He didn't intend to spend the time thinking about building his wall during the procedure. Instead he focused on the unique relationship between his father and grandfather. He loved the tall, controlled man who was his father but he also adored – almost worshiped – his more talkative grandfather. Not given to chatter, Albert Walsh's quiet personality contrasted with the outgoing nature of his grandfather, Harvey. Eric witnessed an easy comradery between the two men. Not only did they work together, but they built their homes side by side and spent many evenings together.

In his younger days, he loved to watch the two together. His mind strayed to when he first started to learn the craft in which they both excelled. Without his permission, his mind drifted back to the wall.

***

Eric stripped off his shirt on sunny days. Muscles in his arms and shoulders awakened and began to cooperate. His hands became acclimated, and the blisters healed after he found the horsehide gloves his father left draped over the wheel barrow.

Soccer continued to shadow him each day, lying beside the trench as he worked or walking beside him as he hunted rocks. Wyn came by a few times. But once he realized the only help he would be allowed to give was hefting stones, and that Eric wasn't interested in hearing about the great walls of history, he didn't stay long. Sometimes Eric felt like Soccer was his only friend.

As the stack of stones got higher, a couple of chipmunks began a daily inspection. Gradually, their number increased until a coterie of tan and brown chipmunks scurried around the rocks like disgruntled building inspectors, twittering their disdain and stomping their disapproval, teasing Soccer into a swift chase. But as soon as the dog went back to his nap, the rodents continued their anti-wall rally.

Eric learned to set his weight by positioning his feet, balancing himself and using thigh muscles when he lifted the larger rocks. His stacks of stones grew steadily and one day he cut stakes and pulled a string line along the proposed route of construction. He intended to work in eight to ten foot segments, digging the trench and laying stones.

He cut a measuring stick and painted a twelve inch measurement in vivid red, and began to dig the footing for his foundation. He dug and dug. Eight feet? He couldn't manage a three foot beginning.

It seemed like he had worked for hours. He had learned not to be distracted by passing cars or squawking blue-jays. He paid little attention when he heard an automobile pull over and a door slam. He was startled by a merry laugh.

"You killing snakes, boy?" Pastor Earl leaned down to pet Soccer.

Eric looked up to see the inquisitive face of Pastor Earl. He thought it was pretty obvious as to what he was doing, and he did not reply.

"No need to go at it like that. Wear yourself out before you get started. You won't get it finished in an afternoon. Need to develop a rhythm."

"I need to dig a trench."

"Let me show you. Okay?" Pastor Earl stepped into the narrow hole and accepted the shovel. He put his foot to it and Eric listened to the crunch as he cut through grass roots. There was a swishing sound as Pastor Earl scooped up soil and flopped it onto the ground. He was so good he made the drudgery look easy.

He sculptured smooth, vertical sides and the small square became rectangular and finally the excavation began to inch forward.

"Need to pace yourself," the old man said. "You'll learn to describe the shape of the stones with your shovel." He demonstrated with a slight indentation in the bed of the trench. "Before long, you'll dream about the bottom contours of your stones." He handed the tool back.

"You'll spend a lot of time staring at each stone, rotating it and memorizing its shape."

Eric grinned. "I already suffer nightmares about the blasted stones."

"You remind me of your grandpa," Pastor Earl remarked casually. "Finest man I ever knew. Loved that man, I did. You know, we started school together. He taught your dad everything he knows and God knows there's not a better craftsman on this planet than your dad." He paused to chuckle and to stroke his beard. "Of course, it took them awhile to work out the kinks in their relationship."

Eric stared at the bearded man.

"Why, I recollect —" But he didn't continue his reminisces.

As much as Eric wanted to prod him on, he had the distinct feeling that pastor Earl had already said more than he had intended to say.

He smiled. "Just take your time. You'll be glad you did it right. You are going to make it just fine, son. But, why don't you make piles of stones along the line of your fence? Save yourself a little effort as you work."

***

As Eric opened the trunk of his car, Joel joined him.

"What do you have there?" Joel asked.

"Ready mix." Seeing the surprise in his brother's face, he explained: "I' m going to try to finish that fireplace and grill. I ordered extra stones to be delivered – in case I need them. Dad and Clay left a nice little supply."

"We wouldn't want you trying to cut through the blackberry briers to Dad's supply, but I've never seen ready mix in a bucket."

"It's a lazy man's way."

"I've thought so many times about how much we could enjoy cooking out for family gatherings and when my band meets for dinner. Let me carry that. Can you feel the effect of the dialysis immediately?"

Eric gave no protest as Joel took a bucket in each hand. "It's a slow process, but dialysis keeps me alive. I met a friend of yours – Lou Ann."

"Did she tell you that she plays a mean banjo?"

"She plays the banjo? She told me she couldn't sing. Does she play with you?"

"Indeed she does. You've got to hear my band! When is Kate coming? We want to plan a concert." He put the buckets in the wheelbarrow Eric had pulled out of the storeroom.

"Kate says she doesn't want to watch me die. She watched her father die."

"None of us wants to watch you die. I wish I had been a match. I'd give *anything* to give you a kidney."

"And I would do the same for you, Joel."

"I know," Joel responded seriously. "By the way, " he continued, "Clay called while you were at the clinic. You don't have to die, you know." He finished the sentence in a quiet voice. He touched Eric gently on the shoulder.

"There are over 93,000 of us

76

on the UNOS waiting list for organ transplants," Eric said quietly, then explained, "The United Network for Organ Sharing is a non-profit, scientific organization that administers organ procurement and transplantation network. They maintain the waiting list and facilitate the procurement for recipients. "

"I was talking about – "

Eric stiffened and Joel removed his hand. "I know what you were talking about. Tell me. If you were needing a transplant – would you allow your daughter to be a donor?"

Joel leaned against the tool shed. He folded his arms across his chest. His voice tone was as low as a bass fiddle. "No, I don't think so. Really, I don't know. I wouldn't want to give up."

"Who's talking about giving up? But only 25,000 to 30,000 on the list will receive a kidney in time this year. I have to be realistic."

"Have you considered it from Clay's viewpoint – no, no," he added hastily. "I won't bug you about it. Kate is doing enough of that."

"Thanks, Joel. Kate is bugging me and Mom is praying for me. Wonder who will win out."

Joel chuckled. "It depends if they're on the same team." He looked up, but he smiled at his taller, younger brother. "We waited to eat lunch with you."

Chapter Ten

"But, Eric ...," his mother questioned, "Can you do the work?"

"I can only tell you what I told Clay. We won't know until I try. I really want to try. Kate made me a protective arm band to protect the fistula."

"I remember. Once you started on that wall, Betsy and I couldn't get you to stop to do anything."

She reminded him that Betsy and her family were coming to supper, and he excused himself to rest in the hammock until the stones arrived.

***

That summer his hair bleached to a pale flaxen color in the summer sunshine and the high altitude contributed to the bronze tan that spread across his face and arms.

His father kept his word. He didn't harass him and, indeed, he indicated no interest at all in the wall – or in Eric.

If hauling material and digging the trench had been difficult, the next phase of the work was worse. He followed Pastor Earl's suggestion and prepared careful indentations to receive the first stones. He examined each one upside down and sculpted its shape into the earth. It was only when he tried to add the second layer that he got into trouble.

Each stone had an irregular shape and none of them would rest neatly on the top of another. He tried using smaller rocks as wedges, pushing them to the back of little gaps and then adding pebbles to make the wall stable. But the configuration was wobbly. He tried wedging the stones against the sides of the trench, but the stones wouldn't stack properly.

He smashed several fingers and uttered words he probably should not have. Soccer would sit up and give him an incriminating stare before dropping back down and curling into his favorite ball position.

Eric chided his dog. "Who's side are you on, anyway?"

Eric made several trips to the church yard to study the wall there. Trouble was, his stones were not flat on top and bottom. He remembered Pastor Earl's advice to ask his father.

As his frustration grew, so did his resentment toward his father. His dad had it easy. He bought his stones from a quarry, and they were probably precut to fit. He also used mortar to hide the irregularities. He had a helper to mix the mortar and another to keep him supplied with neat little mounds of fresh mud. Yet he expected Eric to do the whole job by himself. Perhaps he finally had the answer as to why both his brothers had left the mountains. His father had undoubtedly assigned each of them the task of building a wall. Finally, he reached the end of his rope and swallowed his pride and asked his father for help.

"Are you laying the stone yet?" Mr. Walsh asked.

"No, sir," Eric responded, "but I sure have tried."

His dad chuckled. "After supper, I'll give you a hand."

Gazing down at his pathetic efforts at building the wall, Eric wanted to hide, but his father pursed his lips and nodded. "Sides of the trench straight and smooth. Twelve inches deep. This is obviously not the work of a sissy."

Eric felt tremendous pleasure in response to the kind words. "Pastor Earl helped me get started."

"Pastor Earl? Well, what do you know? He's been around a long time. Helped me once, too."

Eric saw, to his embarrassment, that he had failed to remove a couple of unstable stones he had been experimenting with, but he hoped his dad would notice that he had followed the rule: one on two and two on one. Even in his tentative placements, he had painstakingly put one stone over the break of the first two and two stones over the next stone, alternating the joints.

His dad wriggled a stone with his toe. "Uh, uh," he grunted and Eric could feel his face turning warm.

Mr. Walsh knelt on one knee and laid a small canvas tool bag on the ground. He took out a steel implement he called a pitching tool and a small hammer. Picking up an offending stone, he turned it over, standing it on one of the larger stones, he positioned his tool near the edge. He gave it a few good whacks with his hammer, forming a smooth bed on the bottom of the stone. When he replaced it, the stone cradled itself easily and firmly on the back of the stone in the trench. "I like that better."

Mr. Walsh spent several minutes moving down the row of rocks, sorting, selecting. He would choose one, using his hammer or sometimes only the pitching tool to split or alter a stone into a usable shape before depositing it on the wall.

"They have to sit solidly," he said. "Securely bed the stones to provide a proper base for the next layer. After a while you get a natural swing to the work. You'll be able to distinguish the sounds and know when a stone lands solid, every knob and hollow making contact. Then there will be no rocking in place."

Eric nodded, but he wasn't so sure. It couldn't be that easy.

"Here," his dad said, "you try it."

Eric nervously snatched a stone and clumsily positioned it on the larger stone. Then he turned it over and gave it a resounding whack with the hammer. The stone shattered apart, and the crumbling made a little rustling sound as it hit the other rocks and bounced off. He groaned, but his father said, "Rome wasn't made in a day, nor is a wall. Just takes practice. Use this tool. It has a Carborundum tip brazed to the edge so you can slice a stone. Use the hammer gently."

"I think it's going to take all summer to build this wall."

"All summer? I spent two and a half summers on that wall at the church!"

Eric gawked his astonishment. "*You* built that wall?"

Mr. Walsh smiled. "I was barely fourteen when I started. I remember that Pastor Earl helped me dig the foundation. Told me to ask my dad any questions about the masonry."

"Did you ask your dad?"

"'Course not. Not until I got desperate." They laughed together and some of the tension drained from Eric's shoulders.

The next stone broke more evenly. With only minor adjustments, the third one fit beautifully. Eric took a deep breath.

"You'll learn to listen for a small, soft click. Make sure each stone fits close. And, by the way, son, these are your grandpa's tools. I was saving them for you should you ever need them."

"Grandpa's tools ..." Eric almost couldn't get the words out. "Gee, Dad. Thanks."

His father had never been a demonstrative man, but his smile of approval, as Eric wiped the tools carefully and put them away, spoke for him.

He wished his father had said more – wished he had stayed longer, but he had shown approval. "Isn't the work of a sissy." Eric treasured those words.

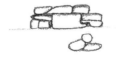

Chapter Eleven

Eric, watching Betsy at dinner with her husband and four sons, felt a lump in his throat. He missed Kate and their children, but also, he was crazy about the little sister who bugged him so much when they were kids. She had suffered though a miserable first marriage, but apparently this union was solid and happy. Bets looked almost as young as her boys: twenty four, twenty, seventeen and fifteen. Russell had adopted the older boys and treated them just like his own. He taught math at Mayland College.

His mother had prepared Eric's favorite squash casserole, and he savored the aroma.

Eric had always enjoyed his nephews. The older ones, Al and Grant, were more serious than their younger brothers, and both were students at Appalachian State University.

The younger boys, Rusty and Harvey, were constantly teasing each other. They were all good looking and well mannered. They were thoroughly enjoying the fried chicken.

"What are you boys studying?" Eric asked, passing the mashed potatoes.

"My bothers are studying girls," twenty-year-old Grant said and clicked his tea glass against Rusty's glass.

Grant, was an undergraduate student, and Al was working towards a graduate degree in business. The two younger boys reported they wanted to be "Cowboys and Indians."

Bets complained. "Be serious, boys. Rusty, you told me that you want to be a journalist."

"Yes. an investigative reporter, but Harve wants to be an artist like you."

Harve, the quietest of the quartet, finally spoke up, "And I'd like to write books like Aunt Kate – only I want to illustrate my own books."

"Uncle Eric," Al said, "I understand you're going to finish the outdoor fireplace and grill. Can I help?"

"I do have a problem. Dad and Clay gathered their stones – and I suspect brought some from the stone yard – but blackberry briers and other vegetation have taken over. I'll have trouble cleaning the mess up. You could help with that. I bought some more. Rocky McKenzie did a great job matching the stones."

"Tell me when to come."

"Okay. I'll have to experiment a little first. Thank you, Al."

Everyone talked about how terrific it would be to have the fireplace for cookouts.

"Then, why didn't some of you finish it?" Eric asked.

"Never thought of it," Joel confessed.

"Me either," Russell agreed.

Eric quipped. "That's the way with you creative people. Mind locked in the fantasy world and you think of nothing practical."

His mom chimed in. "Listen to the artist speaking."

Sherie and Bets started to clear the table, and the two younger boys got up to help.

Harve came back from the kitchen with a chocolate cake that made Eric's mouth water. Bets carried the coffee pot while Sherie and Rusty each carried coffee cups.

"Wow! Some teamwork," Eric said, and Bets smiled. She reminded him that Durrell was coming over on Saturday.

"You could have hired him to finish the fireplace, Joel," Eric said.

"Mom, is Durrell the one Grandpa beat up when he ruined Uncle Eric's picture?"

"What nonsense," his grandmother chided. "Albert never beat anyone up."

"Just threatened to," Betsy said and did a clever imitation. She stood up and placed her hands at her waist, and in a raspy voice said, "You get out of here – off of my property – or I'll get my rifle and blow your head off. And don't come back to work."

Their mom was horrified. "No, Betsy, you're exaggerating. You'll give your sons a terrible impression of their grandfather. Please sit down and eat your dinner."

Sherie laughed. "I've never heard this story! Tell me!"

Betsy put her fork down and leaned back in her chair. She loved telling a good story.

"It was the fourth of July, the year Eric started to high school. We had our traditional picnic, inviting Dad's crew and all the family and neighbors. Eric had worked all winter on a watercolor painting for the summer festival. It was a beautiful cougar. Remember, Mom?"

"Grandmother called it a 'catamount.' I hadn't heard the term in years." Mrs. Walsh turned to her grandsons. "The early settlers called the cougar a 'catamount'."

Betsy continued, "Grandmother swore she could see the cougar's ear twitch in Eric's painting. We had planned a dramatic unveiling. But while everyone else was playing baseball, Durrell slipped into the house and painted the eyes a fire-engine red and painted blood dripping from the mouth"

Eric sipped his coffee quietly before he said. "I was dumb-founded that Dad was so upset by it."

"Oh, he was mad. He went to the toolshed and got some paint thinner, hoping he could get the red off. But, he didn't understand watercolor and just made it worse. He was almost as upset with himself as he was at Durrell, " Mrs. Walsh said. "I guess he was mad enough to thrash the boy, but he didn't threaten him with a gun!"

"Makes a good story, though," Russell said and patted his wife on the shoulder.

***

Eric lay across the bed with the cell phone at his ear telling Kate that he was "rich and famous." He laughed as he told her about Lou Ann.

Kate interrupted. "Is she pretty?"

"Pretty? Let me think. Yes, I guess you'd call her pretty. She has long red hair and lovely legs – I mean eyes." He laughed, enjoying Kate's reaction, knowing full well that he had never given her any excuse for jealousy.

"And Durrell is coming tomorrow. Remember the bully on Dad's crew? I'm not sure I want him to come, but Bets invited him. Perhaps he will help me with the fireplace."

Then, almost as an afterthought he said, "What if I took Clay's kidney and later he became sick?"

"Even if you don't accept it, he could get sick."

After he told her good night, he lay awake a long time. Kate had finished her undergraduate degree and just been accepted for graduate school when her father died. Eric asked her once how she ended up working in the office at the Art Institute.

"There was no money to go on to school and I had to make a living and to help Mom. I needed to do something entirely different – and I loved art. I also learned to love an artist."

He wondered if she had ever regretted losing the boyfriend she had followed to Chicago. He knew the answer. She had been wonderfully happy in their marriage until he became ill. She hadn't even mentioned Clay tonight until he brought the dilemma up.

He turned over. In a determination to push Clay and the transplant from his mind, he focused on Durrell's destruction of his painting and the summer when he was fifteen.

***

Eric was sitting quietly in his room, almost in shock. There was no way he could paint another picture in time for the summer arts festival. He looked up to see his father standing uncomfortably in the doorway.

Eric wanted to ask him what they had done with the painting, but his father didn't say. "I'm sorry, kid."

"That's okay."

"No, it's not okay! Durrell is a dim-witted nincompoop, but I don't know what we can do about the picture. I have come to ask a favor. I'm going to be short handed tomorrow and I am already running behind schedule as usual. I can't afford to lose a good man or two. Durrell has been running my mixer –"

"Dad, I can't work with Durrell."

His father gave him a startled look. "I don't intend that you work with him. I just need you to help man the mixer for awhile. It's a pretty hard job for Mike alone."

"Of course, Dad. Whatever you want."

Mr. Walsh leaned over and touched him lightly on the back. "I'm not sure if Dave will show up either," he said. "He may be too upset because your mother insisted that I fire his brother. Good-night, Eric."

Eric drew a long, deep breath. He couldn't believe his father had fired Durrell because of what he had done to Eric's watercolor.

***

Eric rubbed sleep from his eyes and opened the cab door of the truck at the job site. Old Mike was already there and he gave Eric an inquisitive stare.

Eric helped his dad lift the wheelbarrow from the truck and gather other tools. As he pushed the barrow over to the mixer, he ran his hands along the handles and checked the balance. Fine tool, he thought. A pleasure to use.

Mike's pale blue eyes swept over Eric. "Growed some, ain't you?"

"Hope so. I can keep up."

"Where ya been?"

Eric hadn't expected an inquisition. "Studying," he replied with a grin.

"Studying?" Mike's voice rose in astonishment. "What?"

"Weight lifting."

"Weight lifting?" Mike's eye shifted to Eric's shoulders. He pursed his lips and nodded. "I see."

Eric was amused by the puzzlement in Mike's face. "I've been wrestling with rocks and dancing with a shovel."

Mike scratched his head above his right ear. "You don't say!"

Mr. Walsh leaned over to deposit a bag of mortar mix he had delivered on his shoulder. "You took the wheelbarrow too quickly. You'll need to get the rest of these bags of cement."

Eric spun the barrow around and started back to the truck. He had no desire to carry the bags of cement that weighed nearly a hundred pounds each.

"Where's Durrell?" Mike asked when he returned with the load.

"Don't know." Eric replied and Mike scratched his head just above his left ear.

Eric inspected the progress of the job. They were building a high retaining wall to hold back the mountain from a new shopping center. Bulldozers had cut into the hillside and the wall would prevent mud slides and form the northern periphery for the parking lot.

Mike watched in admiration as Eric hoisted the bags of mix from the wheelbarrow. "Guess you *have* growed!"

Dave pulled into the driveway, and Eric saw the relief on his father's face. Losing both Dave and Durrell could have been disastrous.

Eric hadn't sorted out his feelings about the firing of Durrell. It had amazed him. The fact that his dad had made such a sacrifice put him on notice that he had to make it up some way. Durrell was as strong as an ox and the crew would miss him. Eric would work until he dropped to make up for the loss.

"Think you remember how to do this?" his father asked, and Eric sprang into action.

Mike sliced a bag of mix with sharp stab of his spade.

Eric grinned. "Eighteen shovels of sand to one bag of mix, and about five gallons of water," he recited. He pulled the rope on the gas engine, and the mixing blades began to turn. He shoveled sand into the mixer and added the mortar mix. He dry mixed the ingredients and then pulled the hose over. Eric sprayed water into the drum, and the concoction began to splash and churn.

"Yep," Mike muttered. "You'll do in a pinch."

***

Eric climbed wearily into the truck. It hadn't been an easy day, but he would've given Durrell a run for his money. His shoulders and legs throbbed from fatigue, but he had maintained his endurance during the long hours of heavy work.

From his more deliberate solitary work, he had been thrown into a frenzy of activity. He knew the crew depended on the mortar supply, and he struggled to keep up. During lulls in the operation of the mixer he helped carry stones to the scaffold where his father worked. He took great pleasure in knowing that not once did he keep him waiting. His dad treated him with polite professionalism, just as he did each other member of the crew.

When there was a brief respite, he would watch his father. Mike, seeing his absorption, began explaining: "Your dad is gonna be sorting soon, hunting a stone to use as a 'tie-stone.' That's one that extends through lengthwise the width of the wall. It helps hold both sides together. He'll slowly make the wall more narrow – but you won't be able to tell."

Mike continued, his voice full of admiration. "There ain't a handful of craftsmen like him left. Contractors from all over come to hire him. Heard a man from Charlotte offer him more money than he'd ever seen – guaranteed it – to come to the city to work for him."

"Why didn't he go? We had it hard for a long time. I wasn't very old, but I remember when there wasn't enough flour for biscuits."

"I'll remember 'til my dying day what yer pa said. 'Give a man a family he loves, a job he's proud of, and a view of the mountains and he don't need nothing else'."

Eric turned to stare at the wizened little man. "How come you know so much about my dad?"

"Worked fer him, or his dad, all my life."

During the days that followed, Mike became a chatter-box. Eric discovered that his pet peeve was the summer people who had invaded the Blue Ridge to build "summer houses" and lodges. "We started building some of the lodges around Linville at fifty cents a day."

"But, Mike," Eric protested once, "the resort people brought progress to poor sections of Appalachia."

"*Progress!*" Mike sputtered. "They wanted to build a ten story eye-sore right on the tops of the highest peaks. A bunch of 'ten-cent millionaires' swarmed to our hills trying to avoid the heat of the flatlands. Now we're building a blasted parking lot for a shopping center, and they're making *artificial* snow for skiing. You call that progress?"

Eric had to reload the mixer then.

At the next lull the diminutive helper began to reminisce again. "Yep. Yer pa is a master. I remember when he first started to work. Harvey didn't want his boy to be a mason. They were little more than day laborers then. Wanted him to go to the university in Boone to study architecture."

Eric had been staring off into space, half listening. Now he turned back to Mike. "What did you say?"

"Yer grandpa wanted him to go to the university to make something of himself because people were so poor in the mountains. Warn't much building fer awhile."

They both had to give their full attention to the mixer, but later, Mike continued. "Albert said he wanted to work with his hands. Wouldn't change his mind. Said he couldn't figure out why his dad didn't understand that he was *doing something with his life*."

Eric studied the pleasing dimensions and the smooth lines of his dad's work. The stone fit closely together in a pleasing pattern – small and large stones distributed evenly and none of the overlaps between stones he had seen on other walls. His father had started the retaining wall with a depth of three stones, but narrowed the wall gradually. It was only two stones deep now and Mike told him that the top would have a depth of one stone.

His dad was full of surprises. He wanted to work with his hands? That's what Eric wanted to do. He wanted to use a brush and paper. His dad chose to work in stone, but they were both artists.

***

Freezing mountain winters require serious consideration during the warmer months. "Year-rounders," those residents who stay to weather the winter, spend time repairing roads, cutting and stacking firewood, and stocking up on staple groceries. Before the summer is half over, teachers and students return to school in order to allow for snow days when the busses cannot maneuver slick curves and icy roads.

It was only the tenth of August, but Eric would leave his job the next day. He worried about his father and the crew. Mike would have a hard time trying to mix the mortar alone.

About mid-morning, he looked up to see Durrell heading for the parking lot. He clenched his jaw and felt the familiar sickness in his belly. But Durrell by-passed his area and went straight to the scaffold on which Mr. Walsh worked. Eric saw his father glance down and a moment later, he climbed down to confront Durrell.

"Pathetic, ain't he? Boy is mule-brained," Mike said, "but he works as hard as a mule. Shore does admire yer pa. Cain't help but feel sorry fer him." Mike rattled on. "His dad just got up and left. Ran out on him and his mom. But his brother Dave keeps an eye on him when he works here. It's good for them to work together."

Eric didn't comment, but he watched the debate out of the corner of his eye, although he couldn't hear it. Durrell extended his arms in what appeared to be an emotional plea. Mr. Walsh spread his legs, crossed his arms in the way Eric recognized as his "stubborn mode." He pointed his metal trowel at Durrell, waving it in the air for emphasis. Eric had never seen him so animated. In a few minutes, however, Durrell spun around and stomped off.

Feeling a strange letdown, Eric couldn't understand his disappointment. The last thing he wanted to do was to associate with the overbearing Durrell. Yet, he knew the situation was getting serious. Neither his father, nor Dave, mentioned the incident at lunch, and Eric felt a growing uneasiness as the afternoon wore on. Good workmen were hard to find.

The hours crept by, but just as the work was winding down, Durrell came back. He shuffled past the mixer and walked to where Mr. Walsh was washing up. Eric was cleaning the mixer.

A moment later he found himself staring into Durrell's face. He felt the old irritation rising in his chest.

Durrell cleared his throat and took a deep breath. "Your dad says I can't come back to work unless I apologize to you and I sure need the job." He paused to suck in air. His mouth lost its sullen droop and Eric was amazed to see his lips tremble. "I meant it as a joke. I thought you could paint over the red. I sure need to work."

Eric kept him waiting as he gave the mixer a final spray with the hose. He felt an exhilarating sense of power. "School starts tomorrow," he pointed out.

"I can't go. I have to help my mother and the younger kids." His voice was hoarse.

Eric gazed nonchalantly toward Grandfather Mountain. He would demonstrate his superiority by establishing the fact that he was unimpressed by Durrell's problems. He was, after all, the boss's son. He couldn't resist dangling his advantage in front of Durrell, like an ardent fly fisherman casting into the cold riffles of Doe River. *Let him squirm! Let him plead for this job!* Eric had never been in a position with such command. His dad had given him an unexpected authority and he was going to enjoy every minute. "I'm not sure." He hesitated, savoring the moment. He hoped Mike was appreciating this.

But Durrell failed to squirm. He took a step closer to him and Eric fought the temptation to step back himself. The boy actually looked scared but Eric had enough sense to know he wasn't afraid of *him*. He was terrified of not getting the job.

He said again, "I'd like to work."

A little quiver of shame pushed its way into Eric's mind. If he couldn't accept the apology for Durrell's sake, he should consider his father, Dave and Mike.

"Well, they need you," he said, finally.

Durrell squinted at him a moment. "Then it's okay with you?"

Tolerantly, Eric said. "Yeah. I won't be here."

"Thanks," Durrell said simply. He trudged back to report to Mr. Walsh.

Eric sighed and discontentment washed over him. Suddenly he rammed his right fist into the palm of his left hand. *What a snob! What incredible low-life scum I've become.* His father had stood up for him. Durrell's dad had run out on him. Yet, he had taken advantage of his position to play the high and mighty. He felt about as small as a slimy salamander, slinking under a river rock. He ducked his head in shame and avoided Mike's eyes. He bit his lip.

A few minutes later, Durrell called to Mike as he passed by.

"See you tomorrow."

He didn't look at Eric.

"Yeah," Mike replied. "See ya."

"Durrell!" Eric stopped him and the boy turned back to face him with a questioning look. A worried furrow creased his forehead.

"Glad you're coming back." Eric said.

And Durrell nodded, pressed his lips together in what might pass for a smile and lifted his chin. "Me, too." He didn't assume his usual swagger, but he squared his shoulders as he walked away.

"Yep. Like I said, you'll do in a pinch." Mike affirmed and Eric felt immeasurably better.

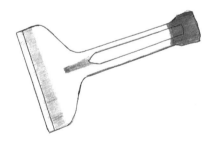

Chapter Twelve

Eric pulled a couple of folding chairs from the tool shed and leaned them against the building. He wasn't looking forward to the meeting with Durrell and was sorry Bets had invited him. His colorful little grandmother had referred to him as, "Dullard Durrell."

Last night, on the phone, Clay had told him to look for his signature. While he waited for his visitor, Eric walked behind the grill to hunt. When they worked together, Clay's grandfather had spread a little mortar on the facing of a back stone so they could leave their signatures. Eric found a blurred thumb print, Clay's initials, ECW. and the date, '92. Next to it was the firm, larger imprint of his father's thumb and the initials AHW. He smiled. When he finished the work, Eric would add his thumb print and initials.

He was sorting through the pile of stones when he heard a truck pull into the driveway. He had worked around Durrell during the summers when he was in high school and college, but they had treated each other with a detached professionalism. He couldn't remember that they had ever had a conversation not related to the job. The only thing they had in common was Eric's father.

Now, he watched the man in his late fifties approaching and realized he looked very much the same – heavy, muscular, with a protruding stomach – except now, instead of faded jeans, he wore tan Carhartt overalls. Even on his day off, he wore rugged work boots. His full beard sported just a hint of gray. He barely glanced at Eric and went straight to the unfinished grill.

"Got a project?"

"A grill and fireplace. Dad and my son were building it, before Dad died," Eric explained.

"He never told me about it." Durrell hitched a thumb into each side pocket, extending his elbows like chicken wings. As he talked, he jabbed the air with his elbows, looking for the world like he was about to take off flying. He looked away and

cleared his throat. "I could of finished it. Yer dad taught me everything I know and gave Dave and me the chance to start our own business." He walked around the grill reverently, as though it were a shrine.

Eric felt a moment of panic, or as his sister Betsy would say, he felt discombobulated. Surely the guy wouldn't start blubbering! He hastened to explain, "It was just a project he started to teach my son to lay stone. I don't think it mattered to Dad whether he finished it or not."

"Wal, he got the firebrick and the angle iron in." He pointed to the yellow brick that lined the interior of the fireplace and grill. "I can identify every stone yer dad set here. Genius leaves its mark."

Eric was running the gamut of emotions this morning. Now he felt defensive about Clay's work. "My son was only about thirteen so, of course you can tell their work apart. Clay is a master craftsman now."

"I believe it!" Durrell's face broke into a grin. "Mr. Walsh told me often enough. He carried a snapshot of you and the boy in his wallet. Did you know that?"

Eric didn't know, and he was touched that Durrell told him.

"Always made me feel left out. I wanted a relationship with my father so bad. Yer dad was the nearest thing I ever had to a father, except for, maybe, my brother Dave."

Both men walked around the work, each pausing to point out specific trowel marks. Eric pointed out the initials and explained: "I was planning to try to finish it, but I'll be self-conscious about my work now that you have pointed out the superiority of Dad's work."

Durrell gave a hearty laugh. "Still got them artist hands? I'll come finish it if you want. Aren't you sick or something like that?"

"Something like that," Eric acknowledged. "But I want to finish it."

Durrell nodded. "I understand. It's a father-son thing. You read about them transplants? I told my wife I wish I could of gave yer dad one."

"Durrell," Eric pointed out, "Dad died of a heart attack. I don't think you could have given him your heart."

"Would of if I could of."

Eric didn't doubt it.

Durrell mused, "Won't take a half day's work." He pointed to the grill. "Won't take but a few hours. That all it'd take me. Longer fer you. Just make sure the chimney steps up and back to draw smoke away."

"Yeah, I know. I'll call you if I get into trouble. I want to thank you for coming by. Come say hello to Mom. She has some coffee and cinnamon rolls ready."

"Mrs. Walsh always was real nice. I'd like to see her again. Mr. Walsh meant everything to me. I tried to be the kind of father he was."

Eric couldn't think of how to respond to such adoration. "So, how is Dave?"

"Dave's retired and living in Mountain City. His wife's family is from there, you know. I've got four young 'uns. Did your dad tell you about my kids?"

"Of course," Eric lied and hoped God would consider it a white lie. "He thought a lot of you, Durrell." That was the truth.

Sitting at the kitchen table with his mother, Eric listened to Durrell brag on his father again. "Mr. Walsh must have been a perfect father. He fired me, you know, when I ruined Eric's picture. My dad never took up fer me."

As soon as Durrell left, Eric returned to the grill. He picked one of the larger stones and turned it over and over in his hands, studying its shape. He tried it several spots near the chimney but realized that this one would require the pitching tool.

Suddenly, Eric felt queasy and opened one of the folding chairs to sit in.

Durrell had told him that he would have given his life for Eric's dad. "I would of if I could of." He was touched by the devotion. "Mr. Walsh must have been the perfect father."

My, how perceptions mislead. How little Durrell knew. Eric wondered what he would have thought if he had known about the conflicts in the household. His oldest brother left home to join the army, much against their father's wishes. Joel left home to become a career musician, against their dad's advice; and Eric really stirred up a hornet's nest when he left to follow his dreams. They enjoyed brief periods of peace but his father had never really accepted his passion, or tried to understand it. Any truce was short-lived. But Durrell's remarks made him realize there were good, honest *noble* attributes in his father also.

He leaned over to hang his head between his knees and supported his head with both palms. He felt totally discouraged. He was beginning to realize that he might not be able to finish the grill.

Eric felt a hand on his shoulder and looked up into the worried expression on Joel's face.

"Are you okay, Eric?"

"I don't know. With failing kidneys, I don't have the energy to work on the project."

Joel pulled up the other chair and unfolded it. "Tell you what. Just postpone it for awhile. Come back and finish it after you have the operation."

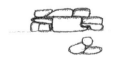

Chapter Thirteen

Few things moved Eric as much as pleasing art, skillfully executed. In his work as Art Director in a sizable publishing firm, Eric had seen some awful stuff submitted as art, some decent art material and some astonishingly exciting work. Seldom, however, had he been as *moved* as he was studying sketches today.

"They are exquisite, Harvey."

"Do you really think so, Uncle Eric? Mom said to show them to you."

Harvey was waiting for him when he woke up from his nap, and Eric recognized the attitude at once. His nephew clutched a brown portfolio close to his chest, and his face registered pride and also a fear of rejection. The wistfulness in his eyes struck home. Eric had felt the same way when he was fifteen.

The portfolio held some finely polished ink-rendered scenes, but the ones that especially captivated Eric were pencil drawings, done spontaneously and quickly. No hesitation or crossovers. "Extraordinary," he said. "I have something upstairs I want to show you."

As Eric started toward the stairs, his nephew said, "Let me go."

"Okay, on the bedside table in my room, there is a folder. Some of my grandfather's sketches."

As the boy started up the stairs, Eric's mother asked, "Is his work any good?"

Eric nodded his head with obvious pleasure. "Some of the best I have ever seen!"

"Better than yours?"

"At his age, yes, considerably better than I could do."

Harvey returned in time to hear the last comment. "I find that hard to believe, Uncle Eric. I know your work." The folder he held really showed its age, yellowed and with the edges frayed. He extended it to Eric.

"You look at them, Harve."

Eric's mother stood up and glanced over Harvey's shoulder. "What are they?"

"I guess you could say that they were the work of my first teacher, Grandpa." Eric turned on another light and the three of them passed the sheets of paper among them.

"They look a lot like mine," Harvey said. "I hope no one will think I copied."

Eric pointed out some similarities. The older sketches had a bit more refinement in the ink renditions, but the pencil drawings looked very much alike.

"Dad said he didn't think art could be taught like, say, math. He thinks you are either born with the talent, or you are not."

"Well, Harve, your father is right, I believe, to some extent. I had a teacher who insisted that anyone can be taught to draw. I don't believe you can create an artist anymore than you can cultivate a beautiful voice in someone who does not have the mental and physical attributes to sing; for example, throat structure. But you can teach a singer to breathe properly so that the gift takes less effort. I think a gifted artist can be influenced by an excellent teacher. An artist might eventually reach his potential without help, but instruction could save a lot of hit and miss disappointments and wasted time."

Mrs. Walsh said, "You didn't take three seconds to recognize Harvey's skill. How did you know so quickly?"

"Look." He pointed to a sketch of a horse, grazing by a fence. "No hesitation. Strong, firm, confident lines. Harvey has his perspective down to a 'T'. I really had to work on that."

His mother wrinkled her nose. "What is perspective?"

Eric nodded toward his nephew. "Tell her, Harve."

"I don't know the formal words, but I think it has to do with size and distance. A man is not as large as a train. You can see that the mountains are large in proportion to the house, even though they are not side by side."

Eric smiled. "He just has artistic instincts, Mom. I guess it must be intuitive. I think we have the potential of a great artist in my nephew!" he said, but Harvey didn't smile.

"Don't mock me, please. I really want to learn."

"I am not mocking you! I *know* how important it is to you because I have been in your shoes. I'll send you a couple of books when I get home, but the main thing I can tell you is to practice, practice and practice." He reached into his shirt pocket. "Try this pencil. It's a woodless one. All graphite. Try to draw big, using your whole arm."

His grandmother laughed. "And by all means, don't lose your sketches at school."

Eric agreed. "Most definitely, don't leave your drawings at school. I did once and it scared me out of three years growth."

"Thank goodness it did," his mother said. "You have to stoop to get through a doorway now."

Harvey looked at each one quizzically. "Why do I feel that a story is coming?"

"Tell her, Eric. Tell her about Miss Leveau."

"One night Dad and I had a heated argument about art classes. It wasn't really an argument, because I wasn't allowed any rebuttal. Dad found out I was taking art in high school and he accused me of not facing my responsibilities. He said drawing was my fantasy, my excuse to avoid work."

Eric described the scene just as he remembered.

***

"You don't need to take art any more than a frog needs instructions on how to catch a fly. Are you going to be like your brother and always avoid reality? Joel hunts wealth, fame and glory. You need to study something useful for crying out loud."

"It's not for glory or fame or money, Dad."

"What is it for? That's what I'd like to know."

Eric glanced out the window. He felt so inadequate. "I can't explain why. I only know I have to paint."

"You have to eat also, and someone has to provide a roof over your head. I'll teach you a trade or help you go to school to learn one, but I will not support your blind obsession for painting your little pictures." Mr. Walsh retorted as he left the room.

Eric couldn't understand the weariness and the disappointment in his father's voice. He took a deep gulp of air. *I will never be able to please him!*

In his room, he toyed with his math assignment, unable to concentrate. Then he picked up his sketch pad. Perhaps he was trying to escape and avoid reality, but he didn't care. He started doodling, just letting his mind and hand go. Before long, he had an amazing caricature of his art teacher, Miss Leveau.

The sketch was not flattering. It was outlandish. But, it was fun!

He drew her nose, accentuating its length and adding an exaggerated helmet-like hairstyle. He enlarged her mouth considerably and made tiny eyes, half concealed by drooping eyelids. Still having fun, he blacked out one front tooth. He gave her a white smock, and changed the contour of her figure to make her top heavy and far more buxom than she really was. Then he gave her boxcar-sized shoes. She was looking toward the ceiling and rubbing her fingertips with her thumbs. "Look up, students, look up!" she instructed in a bubble over her head.

Eric grinned before tucking the drawing into his math book. Then he finished his homework, and went to bed.

It wasn't until he started to show the sketch to Merwyn the next day that he missed it. He prayed all day that he had left it at home.

His caricature of Miss Leveau was not at home, but after a few days of frantic hunting, he relaxed – more or less. He had moments of panic each time she looked at him or paused beside his desk to offer suggestions on his drawings. He found himself scrutinizing her every word, every expression. He searched for signs of sadness or anger. The shame for his portrayal of her increased as his affection and respect for her grew.

One day she surprised him by pinning his drawing of the quarry on the bulletin board and spent part of the class explaining what it was about the sketch that pleased her so much. The assignment was a study in light and shadow. He drew the effects of sunlight on the upper sides of the granite and showed the lower levels, where stone had been excavated, shaded from the sun by the opposite sides of the quarry. Eric was feeling a bit light-headed and possibly a bit cocky when the bell rang but as he started to exit, she asked him to stay in the classroom a moment.

Something about the way she looked at him gave him a pin-prickling premonition that he didn't want to hear what she had to say. "I want to mention something else, Eric. You have unusual artistic ability." She hesitated. "Part of the strength of a great artist is the ability to see people in such a way as to caricature well – and fairly."

She clamped her lips together and her chin trembled and he *knew* she had his drawing. His heart dropped to his shoes when she continued. "Let me say, simply, that a fine artist retains an exemplary sense of decency."

He could feel his face getting warm, and his eyes must have doubled in size.

"An artist may treat his subject with humor, but also with kindness. Cruelty can produce devastating results."

For a moment, his lungs shut down. He lowered his eyes and his chin dropped so far that it grazed his Adam's apple and he was speechless. A chill spread through him.

"That is all, Eric." She dismissed him and walked away, giving him no chance to apologize.

He stumbled from the classroom. He wondered how long she had known about his drawing of her. She had praised his work, complimented him on his skills, all the time knowing he was a louse!

Chapter Fourteen

After Eric shared his experience with Harvey, he continued to think of his high school days, and especially his friendship with Merwyn McNeil. That night, his memories kept him awake.

***

"So, you have been building that dumb wall all summer." Merwyn whipped out a red bandana from his hip pocket and carefully dusted the seat next to Eric. He sat down and the school bus jerked into action.

"I noticed that you didn't come around, except to annoy me." Eric said.

"Looked like work, man. And you wouldn't take my suggestions."

Eric spread out his fingers and examined his hands. He pointed out several callouses to Merwyn. "It *was* work, man," he said, imitating Wyn's speech pattern.

Wyn had lived down the road from the Walshes as long as Eric could remember. They used to spend the summers "hanging out" together. "I'll tell you what I would have done. I would have told my dad, 'If you want that wall built, do it yourself'."

"Yeah. Sure you would." It was no wonder that Grandma had always referred to him as 'Windy Wyn', Eric thought. "And what did you tell your stepdad that you wouldn't do this summer?" he asked.

"Well, I'll tell you! I said to the Mountain Man. I said –" He gave Eric a sheepish grin. "That's different. He isn't my real dad.

But we built the garage."

After his father's death, Wyn's mother married a giant – at least that was the way it seemed to Eric. He stood six feet and nine inches in his stocking feet and weighed over three hundred pounds. Eric had always liked him, but Wyn was less accepting. He resented his role in the family and refused to address him as dad.

Unfortunately, Wyn had inherited his natural father's build. Starting high school, he was straining to reach five feet, two inches. He made up for his Bantam size by becoming the world's most accomplished braggart. Sometimes it was irritating, but Eric had learned to ignore the bluster most of the time.

They had freshman math together and also driver's education. The fact that they shared the latter bothered Eric, but they had arranged it that way so that they could carpool on rides home when the driving part of the class started.

Occasionally, Eric was embarrassed by his friend's behavior. He didn't intend to eavesdrop, when he got to driver education early one morning, but he heard an exchange between Windy Wyn, and Mr. Donaldson.

Wyn was in good form, and his pretentious airs made him hilarious with the right audience.

"I have been in your class for several weeks. Do you know who I am?"

Mr. Donaldson looked up from the opaque projector he was adjusting. He looked puzzled. "Merwyn McNeil?"

Wyn gave an exasperated sigh. "You used to date my mother."

The teacher smiled. "Oh! Are you Dora's boy?"

"No! My mother is Stella."

"Stella? Oh, yes, Stella. How is she?"

Wyn took off his jacket and folded it carefully. "She's fine. After Dad died she married the Mountain Man, Homer Jaynes."

Mr. Donaldson moved back to his desk. "Homer Jaynes is a fine man. I worked with him when he was captain of the rescue squad. I didn't know your father."

"And I have two half sisters." Wyn continued but Mr. Donaldson didn't look especially interested.

103

"Half sisters?"

"Yeah, half girls and half tigers!" Wyn laughed so uproariously that he gave the impression to students just arriving that the teacher had shared an intimate joke with him.

Poor dork, thought Eric, he should stop while he's ahead.

But Wyn continued to dominate the class discussion. "Mr. Donaldson, do you know what I believe?" He didn't wait for reply. "I think that considering the ecology of this world, we should just do away with cars and other equipment that pollute the environment."

Mr. Donaldson seemed to Eric to command extraordinary patience. "Do away with automobiles? Then, Wyn, are you saying that you want to withdraw from this class?"

"No, sir, but I suggest that we all should be worried about the environment and conservation."

***

Strange that Eric would think about Merwyn tonight. He wondered if the family still lived in Avery County. He would have to ask Bets if she was still friends with Wyn's sister, Violet.

Homer Jaynes tried hard to be a father to Wyn. It took the dramatic climax on that horrible spring evening at the quarry to – but Eric refused to consider that experience tonight. Memories always invoked the sounds of sirens, the smell of police flares, the stinging pain in his shoulder and the flashing strobe lights on the belly of the helicopter as it was lifting from the parking lot, like a reborn pterodactyl, blades whipping the air, taking Wyn away.

With determined willpower, he focused his mind on Clay as a toddler. One Sunday afternoon Clay brought a tiny tin "friction" car to him. It cost only a few cents but the child loved it. Someone had stepped on it and flattened it like a dime. "Fix it, Daddy," the three year old said, with complete confidence.

Eric held the piece of tin in his hands and grieved with his son. "It cannot be fixed, son."

That story had a happy ending because he was able to buy him a new one the next day.

The memory of another car invaded his thoughts, unwelcomed.

One night last week he stood beside a rented Cavalier and saw the right front wheel spinning in space.

Why hadn't God just taken him home that night?

How easy it was to give gifts to Clay and Kathy. He and Kate had done something right. Both of their kids were loving and appreciative. Kate always bought treats for the guests at their birthday parties, putting the emphasis on what they gave rather than the gifts guests brought. "It is more blessed to give than to receive." She taught them well.

Perhaps too well.

"Dad. I want to do this." Clay had begged. "With all my heart, I want you to let me be the donor. I have done the research and I know the risks."

"Think about Jane. Your wife and children need to be in on the decision."

Clay sighed. "Dad, we have been through this before. They want me to do this."

"Just think of the logistics, son. How could you miss six or eight weeks of work?"

"I'm the boss, Dad, and I've already discussed this with my crew. It might be only three or four weeks away from the job. My men can manage. They're excited about my doing it and want to have a part in it."

Eric thought, *I'm glad someone is excited about it. I'm not.*

Why wasn't the case reversed? Had Clay needed the kidney and he was a perfect match, he wouldn't be able to get to the hospital fast enough.

But, if Clay needed a kidney it would mean that he suffered the terrible kidney disease that Eric lived with every day. No way did he want his son to face that.

He went to the window and looked out. The house was built so it faced a hollow that opened up the space and gave them a spectacular view. He could see the faint glow of the lights of Banner Elk.

He opened his suitcase, eventually, and found a pill to help him sleep. What he needed, he thought, was Kate. Hundreds of nights she had held him and loved him and helped soothe the anxieties.

However, recently, things had changed. She wasn't as understanding. She wanted him to consider Clay's offer.

"I only want you to live," she whispered.

Eric climbed back into the bed. *Couldn't argue with that wish,* he thought.

Chapter Fifteen

Eric loved the early morning when the house was cool and quiet. He loved having it to himself, to share with his mother and with Princess. He woke when Sherie and Joel left for a performance in North Wilkesboro, leaving him to enjoy the home place with his mother. She was dressed in a simple duster, ironed of course, as she had been every Sunday morning of his memory. He automatically checked his shoes – almost headed for the back porch – but decided they could pass muster this time without shining. He remembered many Sunday mornings as a child, gathered with his older brothers around the big wooden box.

"Did you sleep well, son?" She greeted him as he joined her in the kitchen.

"Once I got to sleep. I finally took a sleeping pill, around two."

She considered him over the rims of her glasses as she poured him a cup of coffee. "But, generally, you're feeling okay? I wondered if the dialysis clinic here is as good as the one in Westchester."

She was busy mixing a cake. The cocoa tin and her flour and sugar canisters were open. "I've mixed the dry ingredients, and while the oven is heating, I can sit down to have coffee with you."

He sat down and leaned over to pet Princess. His mother was keeping the dog's coat combed and brushed; it felt like silk. "This clinic is excellent. Most of them are. I am so grateful for the dedicated health-care people I meet. It must be discouraging."

"What do you mean by that? They must realize that they are helping to keep you, and many others, alive."

"I'm doing so much better than many of the patients. The hardest thing about the clinic is that you see so many people who are worse off than you are. You can't help the sicker ones and you wonder how long it will be until you are in their condition. You just get to know someone and – then, they're gone."

His mother sat across the corner of the table from him and touched his hand. "You've only been on dialysis for about six months, haven't you? Do you know how long most people have the treatment?"

Eric stirred his coffee, then wondered why he had put a spoon in it. He drank it black. He laid the spoon down carefully, trying to avoid coffee stains on the tablecloth. "I'm not sure. I know people who've had dialysis for years. God," he said, "I couldn't take that."

"I believe you could, if you had to."

"I'm not sure, Mom. It's about to cost me my marriage."

His mom's eyes grew wide with alarm. "Surely," her voice sounded stressed, "you don't mean to say that Kate would leave you if you continue to need the dialysis."

He smiled and shook his head. "You don't have to actually walk out on a marriage when you know that it's strained and may only get worse. When it gets that bad, it might as well be over."

"What can you eat today. Eric?" She stood and turned to the stove. "Kate called me yesterday. She's so worried about you I cannot imagine that she feels the marriage is over. She told me you won't live without a transplant."

"She is right, of course. Mom, I am on one list and as soon as I get back, I will inquire about other lists." He knew he sounded irritated, and he was sorry. "Then we will be chained to the cell phone even more – jumping through hoops with blood tests and reevaluations every month to remain on each list. Our life has been in turmoil and it's been hard on Kate. I just can't get by the wall that has come between us."

She didn't complain about his temperament. Sweetly she asked again, "What do you want for breakfast?"

"I'd love some of your pancakes. But I hate to put you to so much trouble."

"Why not? We have time before church." She put her arm around him, leaned over, and laid her head next to his. She smelled of talcum powder and cologne that reminded him of lilacs.

He didn't want her to move away. He thought for a minute that he was going to get weepy. His support group told him to enlist the emotional support of his family. He hadn't shared with his mother how very sick he was. He always downplayed the critical elements. This morning, he wondered if she knew how fast his body was deteriorating. He hated to think about what another family death would do to her.

She stood on her tiptoes to reach up to a top shelf to pull out the green bowl she used to mix pancakes. Always before, she had asked him to retrieve it.

When she brought his plate, piled high with pancakes, she said, "We still have some of the maple syrup that you and Kate sent us last year. I know your diet does not allow bacon. How about more coffee?"

"No more coffee, please. I have to limit my liquids while I am on dialysis – especially on the weekends." He reached around her waist, pulled her close to him and kissed her tenderly on the cheek. There was another time when he desperately needed the emotional support of his mother – and his father. He knew, all at once, that this morning he couldn't ignore the nightmares of that terrible spring evening, before he had much experience with tragedies . The same nightmares kept him awake last night and he must face them during the daylight hours.

"Let me get this cake in the oven. It's your favorite Devil's Food."

"I had nightmares last night about the quarry."

"Oh, yes, the quarry. When they were dynamiting that one near us, the blasts would make the whole mountain shake! Grandma would shake her fist and yell, 'You yellow hard hatted idiots! You are scaring my hens and they won't lay eggs'."

Eric could see his grandma in her chicken pen, trying to soothe her hens.

"Dad would say, 'Now, Ma, our work depends on the quarry.

109

We have to have stones'." She broke two eggs into the big green mixing bowl. "And the dust! Those huge dump trucks would rumble by here, carrying granite slabs as big as a truck – and Grandma would yell, 'Wish you had to dust my house – just once!'"

Eric said, "Ed used the abandoned quarry for target practice."

Mom took a small piece of wax paper and rubbed her cake pans with butter. "Joel said it was a natural amphitheater and rehearsed his guitar there."

"He said the granite provided an acoustic laboratory."

Mom dusted the pans with flour and, tapping the sides, knocked the extra off into the sink.

The quarry became a sanctuary for Eric. He could mourn his grandfather's death. When he sketched, he could coax the image of a gray fox out of the pewter-colored ledges. By moving his pencil he could make an eagle soar, dip into the murky waters and climb into the heavens again, a trout dangling from his talons.

Mom poured in the liquid mix and stirred, and he smelled the vanilla. She shoved the cake into the oven. "Want to clean the bowl and lick the spoon?"

Suddenly he was a teenager again.

***

Eric was painting when his grandmother called up the stairs.

"Eric! This dog of yours has gone crazy! Can you come shut him up?"

As he hurried down the stairs, he could hear Soccer barking frantically and clawing at the back door. When Eric opened the door to let the dog in, he turned and ran toward the road, still barking. Eric stared at Soccer, puzzled. *He is trying to get me to follow him.* "Grandma, where's Betsy?"

"She and Violet took their bikes up the side road."

Eric's heart skipped a beat. That was the way to the quarry, and the girls had asked him earlier to take them there. His dad would hold him responsible! Told him to take care of his little sister. Dad's darling daughter. If anything happened to her his dad would have his skin. How come she needed a babysitter – she was ten years old?

Soccer was turning in circles and barking his head off. Again, Eric opened the door and again the dog started off up the road. "I've got to follow him!" He grabbed his coat and found his dad's truck keys hanging on the nail near the back door. "Grandma, quick! Come with me."

Grandma ran to the truck, and he leaned across the passenger's seat to open the door and gave her a hand so she could pull herself up into the high cab.

Eric had never driven the truck, but he had watched his dad carefully. He ground gears a couple of times before he got the truck into reverse and backed into the road. Soccer waited long enough to see if he was following, then took off up the road.

Eric jammed the truck into gear and headed up the road that led to the abandoned quarry. He had to get those kids home before his father found they had gone there. He drove up the dirt road like the whole U.S. Cavalry was after him.

Eric stomped his foot on the accelerator and the truck lunged forward, throwing both of them back against the seat. Soccer ran ahead. He had quit barking.

"Eric, slow down!"

"They went to the quarry!" He swung the truck to the right, avoiding a big puddle of mud and ice. He could hear the ice cracking in shady sections of the road. He didn't slow down when the road narrowed to two narrow ruts. He slammed the truck into a lower gear and continued his reckless, perilous speed around the mountain.

Finally, they came to the quarry roadway. When they saw two pink bicycles, leaning against a rhododendron bush, his fear found a focus. Beyond the bikes was the old safety fence at the top the quarry. He skidded to a stop near where the truck ramp used to be. They threw open the doors and ignoring the "No trespassing" sign, both of them ran toward the rim.

The top of the quarry had been formed by dynamiting the top

of the mountain and blasting blocks of granite from the side. It was shaped like a huge funnel that narrowed at the bottom of the deep excavations. Mountain springs trickled down the rocks to feed the pit and it was filled with algae covered green water in the summer. During the winter, the frozen surface was littered with ice shards that had fallen from the towering rocks.

Soccer whined and ran ahead to a weed and rock strewn deer tail that led down toward the rim. Eric could see the footprints in the snow; ice crystals were reforming on the melted surface as the sun dropped low against the horizon. His scalp prickled and a big knot formed in his throat. Something terrible had happened. "Grandma, you wait here."

"Give me the truck keys."

"You can't drive!"

"Could-forty-fifty years ago. Give me the keys! Don't argue, boy. I might keep her in the wrong gear all the way, but I'll get help."

***

Now discussing it with his mother, after all these years, he shivered. "I think I would have died if I had allowed anything to happen to Betsy – even if she had slipped off from me.

"And Grandma did get help," Mom reminded him.

"Yes. I managed to get down to the girls on a ledge about fifteen feet down. Betsy had hurt her ankle and had a bad bump on the head. Vi was fine.

"I could hear the wail of the rescue squad siren and we could see headlights sweep across the top rim of the quarry. I didn't know until they got us to the top that Homer Jaynes and Wyn were there. I hated to face Mr. Jaynes because I was afraid he would blame me for Vi's going to the quarry. And I thought that if I had let those girls down, I couldn't stand it."

Mom patted his hand. "All's well that ends well."

"But, it didn't end there, Mom. Wyn and I got to horsing around."

***

The evening was taking its toll. Eric's knees felt like cardboard. He had to find a place to sit before he just folded up, but if Wyn touched him, he'd sock him.

Soccer pushed through the crowd, at that moment. The dog hesitated; then, running, hit Eric like a white thunderbolt. Eric fell against Wyn and they both toppled on the loose rubble like dominos standing on end.

"Watch –" Wyn screamed but, he never finished his sentence. As he struggled desperately for a foothold, the quarry simply swallowed him.

Eric froze. He heard the scrapping of gravel and a crash of tumbling stones below and pandemonium around him. He sank down and vomited on an ebony rock.

Chapter Sixteen

Eric's mother sat down across the table from him. "When we got here, it looked like the whole mountain was covered with fire-engines and police cars, and we were frightened to death. Your dad couldn't even speak, he was so scared," she said. "I thought the house was on fire."

"I don't want to ever go through another night like that. I didn't know you had gotten home from Joel's concert in Charlotte soon after the rescue squad arrived."

"We followed a fire-engine up the road."

"I never saw anything like it, Mom. Mr. Jaynes wouldn't listen to the captain. He demanded the ropes, and he stepped ahead of the First Responders, going down first, while the captain yelled he was going to have him arrested."

Mom laughed. "Sounds like Homer."

"It seemed like forever before I heard someone on the emergency radio was saying his father found him." Eric shook his head. "When they brought Wyn up in the stokes basket, I thought he was dead. I heard the captain order a med-evac helicopter. My skin was wet and clammy like a fish. I watched the copter lift from the ground, white spotlights on the belly. It rose away from us like a mighty dragon bird, a red light on one side and a green one on the other side. It moved backwards, toward the quarry, made an arc and swept back over us, heading toward the sunset. I had never felt so alone. Wyn had his *stepfather* defying everyone to rescue him."

"And you didn't have your father or mother."

"But you came. You both hugged me and Dad didn't scold me. He took me to the ambulance."

***

"I'll go with you to the emergency room and we will get a report on Betsy and Wyn"

It wasn't like the movies in which the ambulances speed through the mountains, skidding around dangerous curves with sirens screaming like cougars. The ambulance descended cautiously through the canyons toward the hospital, and it traveled quietly.

His father sat in the front seat, and Eric was so glad to have him there. Eric turned his head to stare out the dark window. The black outlines of the trees and the lights on buildings became less blurred as they slowed down approaching the hospital.

Betsy had been admitted for observation and treatment for her broken ankle. Wyn was in surgery. In the emergency room. an efficient staff treated Eric's shoulder and stitched up a nasty cut on his thigh where he had fallen on a jagged rock. His dad pushed him in a wheelchair to the waiting room to wait for a report on Wyn.

"It was my fault," Eric confessed stoically.

His father said, "You may not want this, but I'm going to give you some very important advice. You will *ruin* your life if you spend the rest of it worrying about tonight."

"But you weren't there, Dad. We were knocking each other around."

"I know a great deal more than you think I do." Eric's father seemed suddenly very tired. He let his head fall between his legs and braced it with his hands. When he started talking again, his voice was hushed. "I was just about your own age when my cousin and I slipped off to swim in the quarry. We too, were scuffling around and he fell in. He never came up. By the time I was able to get help, he had drowned. His body was caught on some debris at the bottom. Now, you know why I hate quarries and forbade you to go near one."

Eric didn't try to respond. He looked at his dad, wishing he knew how to comfort him. He dozed and woke up with a start.

"How was Joel's concert, Dad?"

"Fine," Mr. Walsh replied. "But my guess is that your mother will regale us for months about how glorious that concert was." He laughed. "Joel sends his love."

All night long he was aware of the quiet presence of his father. Every once in awhile, Mr. Walsh would go check on Betsy and their mother, but he returned to remain with Eric during the long night that seemed never to end and was so filled with uncertainty and fear, and sadness.

Eric drifted back to a troubled sleep. He realized that they had given him something in the emergency room to make him woozy. Later, he woke up and sat staring at his father who had leaned his head back against the wall with his eyes closed. Eric was grateful he had stayed with him. Just watching his dad filled him with tenderness. Eric felt all weak inside and when his dad opened his eyes sleepily, Eric was embarrassed as though looking at him had awakened him. Out of the blue he asked, "Dad, what made you decide to build that wall at the church?"

Mr. Walsh chuckled. "I didn't decide to build it. Your grandpa decided for me. He said I needed to do some hard work. Needed to be willing to get my hands dirty, he said. Learn a trade – discipline."

Eric grinned. "Sounds familiar. Grandpa sure did a good job making you into a great stone mason."

"Once I learned, I never wanted to do anything else for a living."

"Dad, I wish I –"

"Son, it's okay."

Eric nodded and slipped back into sleep. He woke up stiff and sore from the night in the waiting room. Gray clouds in a whitening daylight were blowing slowly across the sky above the mountains.

"Eric?"

"Yes, sir!" He strained to stand up but sank weakly back into the chair. Homer Jaynes filled the doorway.

"He's out of recovery. They've taken him to his room."

"Is he okay?"

"We hope so, he has a concussion and a broken shoulder. He'll sleep until this afternoon. Let me take you home."

"My dad's here. He must have gone to get some coffee."

"Thanks for staying, son. I understand that Betsy's being released. Go on home."

Wyn never referred to his step-dad again as Homer. His new relationship with his dad bordered on hero worship.

Chapter Seventeen

"**Merwyn's injuries** healed, didn't they?" Eric's mother said when they finished talking about the quarry. She placed her hand over his. "It was a terrible experience for you."

"Yes, but why couldn't things have stayed that way between Dad and me?"

"You grew up. You grew up and left him. He didn't want that to happen."

Eric smiled. "I can understand wanting to keep your kids close to you, but I wanted mine to follow their dreams. I don't think Kathy could have been happy had she not been allowed to go to vet school, and Clay wanted to emulate his grandfather."

"Then," his mom replied, "you learned from your father's mistakes. Something good came from it."

They finished their coffee quietly.

"Well, Mom, I guess I had better get cleaned up for church. Can I help you with the dishes?"

"They'll be here when we get back." She ran water in the sink over the bowls. "I need to hurry to get ready myself."

***

Eric looked around the little church he had attended until he left home. Rock, inside and out, it was a beautiful study in traditional mountain architecture. This ceiling was finished with rafters and perlins that supported hundreds of small tree branches. "A walk in the woods," Eric said to himself. As a child he would look up and count the branches. They were jammed close against each

118

other, providing a solid covering. If this service was too dull, he could resort to that technique to stay awake again.

The blueish-gray granite kept worshipers cool in the summer and provided a buffer from the wind during the winter – but little warmth. The old pot-belly stove, that had struggled to warm the church for decades, had been replaced with a modern heating system. As a child, he always wore a coat to church in the winter. The new air conditioning made him glad of his jacket in the middle of summer.

Eric never asked how much his grandfather had contributed to the building of the church. He just assumed that the building had always been there, like the mountains that produced the stones to build it. He felt sure, now, the building was his grandfather's handiwork.

Eric and Kate had neglected church attendance since the children left home. He tried to blame it on his health, but he suspected that he was just plain lazy. Kate continued to attend for awhile without him. He desperately wished Kate was here today.

Eric liked the young pastor, Pete Sands, who supported his family as a salesman at one of the large building supply stores in Boone. He was tall and lean and neatly groomed with short brown hair. Eric guessed he was an athlete. It seemed to Eric, however, that Brother Earl should be filling the pulpit.

Eric was also pleased that the pianist played the hymns joyfully, if not with total accuracy. He hated funeral-like music at church. Perhaps here he could enjoy a short respite away from the nagging awareness of impending death. Apprehension had become a stalking villain – not because he was afraid of death – but because he was responsible for a certain amount of control over death with his ability to either accept or reject Clay's kidney.

As the pastor stood up to preach, Eric was glad that he had an aisle seat that gave him room for his long legs. He stretched them out and prepared to let his mind drift about with his own problems – or to count the branches in the ceiling.

"I am preaching today about life. Jesus said, 'I am come, that you might have abundant life.' But what is life? Why are we encouraged to embrace it, to savor it, and to make the most of our lives? I am reading from the New International Version. Psalm 16:

'I praise the Lord, who counsels me; even at night my heart instructs me.

Therefore, my heart is glad, and my tongue rejoices: my body also will rest secure, because you will not abandon me to the grave, nor will you let your Holy One see decay.

You hath made known to me the path of life;

You will fill me with joy and your presence, with eternal life'."

But what was life without Kate? How could he "embrace" life without her support?

Eric remembered the joke about the deacon who complained that the preacher had gotten too personal. He said that the preacher had "quit preaching and gone to meddling." If meddling meant he had gotten too close for comfort, this one had hit a home run. Was he expected to believe that God would counsel him and tell him what to do about Clay's offer?

He wished he could talk with Brother Earl. What would the old fellow say if he had told him that the doctors wanted to cut open his own son, take a kidney out and install it in Eric? The whole process sounded savagely barbaric.

Eric leaned back a little. *Wonder if Mom will notice if I start counting the branches. I must remember to count silently. I'll start at the front wall and count backwards. I got to four hundred and six when I was about ten years old. One. Two. Three ...*

Could God instruct him? Would He? Was this a promise from the Deity that He would be moved to the top of the City Hospital organ transplant waiting list? Eric knew one person who was on three waiting lists. He planned to investigate other lists as soon as he got home.

Then, in spite of himself, his attention was caught by the pastor who was telling a personal experience. Eric wondered what it had to do with the rest of the sermon, and was sorry he had not paid better attention.

"For several years, I have enjoyed kayaking around the North Carolina Outer Banks. My small craft has taken me to the Swash

Inlet on Portsmouth Island, that I planned to visit one summer morning, leaving Cedar Island just before dawn."

Eric loved kayaking and had visited the Outer Banks soon after graduating from high school. Pete Sands was no sissy if he could paddle a sea kayak to Portsmouth Island.

He continued, "My twelve mile paddle to Swash Inlet would be over open water, and several tiny islands would serve as waypoints along the route. My first waypoint was Harbor Island, right in the middle of Pamlico Sound, about five miles distant.

"My next waypoint was Wainwright Island, barely visible about two miles to the northeast. Shell Island was the next waypoint.

"When I reached the sound side of Portsmouth Island at Swash Inlet, I unloaded the kayak and set up camp. The wind had increased by this time, and it took patience to set up and anchor my lightweight tent.

"My campsite was located about ten miles south of Portsmouth Village. I had achieved my goal of reaching one of the most isolated areas of the Outer Banks.

"I was awakened at daybreak by light raindrops pelting my tent. Weather conditions often change rapidly in this region. I ate breakfast and packed my craft for a return voyage to Cedar Island. Not wishing to carry any more weight than necessary, I dumped

most of my drinking water.

"I retraced my route, making good time until I reached the last leg of the trip – a five mile stretch of water between Harbor Island and Cedar Island. The wind and waves had increased substantially, and the waves were now crashing over the bow of my sea kayak. Seawater had infiltrated both storage compartments of my kayak. The opposing wind made it difficult to maintain my course, and my kayak almost flipped over twice.

"Panic was not an option, but the situation had my full attention. I always considered myself able to control any situation, but here in the middle of the Pamlico Sound, I was approaching exhaustion. I could no longer exercise control over my body. I realized that no one was going to come to my rescue.

"I was going to drown. I did something I had not done in a long time. I prayed. I told God that I was placing myself under His care. I had reached the end of my strength, but I was now in the hands of the master of the wind and waves.

"My physical energy depleted, I allowed my kayak to be turned by the waves. The waves and current directed my course toward Hog Island. The waves were breaking across my back, but the kayak continued to float as an unseen hand steadily pushed me toward dry land.

"Reaching the safety of Hog Island, I collapsed onto the sea grass and lay still. It was now about 2 p.m. and I had been paddling continuously since 7 a.m. I had one liter of drinking water left.

"I discovered an old cabin on this small, uninhabited island with a cistern on the roof. Turning one of the valves, I was rewarded with a stream of clear rainwater. What are the odds of being blown onto a deserted island and being presented with both shelter and water?

"I washed my salt water soaked cell phone and then placed it in the sun to dry out. It worked! I had enough signal to call home and let my family know I was safe. After I talked to my son, David, I did something else I had not done in a very long time – I cried. I cried from the depths of my soul, completely exhausted. I thought about my wife and boys and what my death would have done to them.

"I launched into the mouth of the bay before daylight. The sun was just visible in the eastern sky as I reached my destination, the little boat ramp in Lola.

"All my life I had believed in my ability to make things happen. I was in control," Pete Sands continued. "It wasn't until I was in a situation where I could not control the sea that I was able to admit to myself that I was not ultimately in control of my life. For some of us, the road to faith is a long journey. Faith is indeed a gift from God.

"I would have drowned in the sound had I not trusted God to provide for me. I got into a position of acute need, and let Him take control of my life."

Reverend Sands caught Eric's eye as he concluded: "Your life matters – to God and to your family and to others. You were carefully crafted by the Master. Trust God to provide for you. Trust Him and He will fill you with joy and His presence."

As Eric left the church, one thought followed him to the car. "My life matters to others."

***

Soon after lunch, just after Eric went to his room, Kathy called him on his cell phone. "Did I wake you up from your nap, Dad?"

"No. But, if you had, it would be worth it just to hear my little girl's sweet voice." He sat down on the bed and pulled his tie off.

She laughed. "Dad, I thought you were pro-life."

"Oh, oh. I know exactly where you are going, kiddo. I am pro-life, and I cannot allow Clay to risk his life for me."

"Just hear me out, please. It might seem that I am being awfully selfish, and I don't want to put Clay in danger either, but he is a health nut and in such good shape that I'm sure he will do fine. Dad, I need you to be around awhile."

"I intend to be around for awhile, honey."

"Among other things, I need you to be around to help me with my daughter!"

Eric could see her tossing her blond pony-tail which seemed perfectly in style for a young veterinarian. He could imagine her radiant face and knew she was smiling that huge heart-stopping smile of hers. She had wanted children so badly. "Your daughter?"

123

he asked. "Are you sure it's a girl, Sweetheart?"

"Paul wanted a boy at first, but the sonogram is quite clear. I plan to call her Erica."

Eric stood up and walked to the window, changing the phone to his other ear. "Now, don't hang that label around the poor kid's little neck!" He was tickled to death and he was sure the timbre in his voice told her so.

As he put his phone back into the charger, he thought, *My life matters to Kathy.* Was this what the pastor meant? That my daughter cares enough about me to name her unborn daughter after me? Eric hadn't thought much about seeing his grandchildren grow up.

 The last time he saw Clay's children, Tim said, "Come run with me, Granddad!"

Run? Eric could hardly walk a block, without stopping to rest. If he got a new kidney, he would be able to run with his grandchildren!

Kathy started running in junior high just as Clay had. Since Eric had to catch an early commute to the city, Kate ran with them. She ran with Clay until he left home and continued to run with Kathy until she left for college.

Maybe he could have another chance to run – at least with his grandchildren. He felt great longing to live to enjoy Tim, Valerie and Erica. "Please, God," he prayed.

Kate called. "Darling, I'm coming tomorrow." His heart skipped a beat.

"I'm tired of waiting," she continued. "I thought that if I stayed away long enough, you would accept Clay's gift. But, if you have to do it your way, I'll not have much time with you and I want to share every minute God grants us."

"I mean that much to you?" he asked.

"You know you do. To me and to Clay and to Kathy – just for starters. I just wish you weren't so darn stubborn and cared as much for us as we do for you."

"I am glad you're coming, Sweetheart." That was putting it mildly.

Chapter Eighteen

Sunday evening, Joel pulled his big recliner out of the corner of his office. "Sit here, Eric, and you can see all the action. I'll want you to meet everyone as they arrive. We'll be short a couple of players, but they will be with us at The Pass on Friday night."

Moments later the first musician arrived. "This is Snuffy Belcher, our old man of the band, who plays the best guitar you'll ever hear."

"*Gee-tar,*" Snuffy corrected. "I'm the old gray-headed great grandfather." He bowed low and lifted his hat. He was as bald as a marble.

Eric asked, "How long have you been playing, Snuffy?"

"Bought my first 'gee-tar' from Monkey Ward when I was twelve. Paid two dollars, forty-two cent for it. I guess that was about 1940."

Sherie raced to the door to open it for Cleg Wiseman who was lugging in a large bass violin. As he introduced him, Joel said, "Not all the mountain bands are lucky enough to have a bass fiddler. We have a drummer too, but he couldn't make it tonight." He stepped toward the door to welcome other arrivals but turned back to Eric to say, "Cleg plays the harmonica, also."

Cleg nodded self-consciously and ducked his head, grinning. Later Eric could not recall a single word that Cleg uttered all evening.

Lou Ann Puckett, with her friend Darlin Scuggs greeted Eric next. He knew he ought to stand up, but the recliner felt too comfortable. "We are a diversified group," Joel explained. "Many of my musicians play several instruments. Did you bring your mandolin,

125

Lou Ann?"

Lou Ann had both her banjo and her mandolin. Darlin carried a violin case.

Joel pulled out his guitar. After a few minutes of turning pegs and plucking strings, the instruments were tuned and Joel asked Lou Ann to start the evening chording on her mandolin, playing lead. Then the band burst into *Old Joe Clark* with Joel singing. Eric remembered that song:

"Wished I had a nickel, wished I had a dime,
Wished I had a pretty girl to kiss and call her mine."
The rest of the band joined in on the chorus, singing with gusto.
"Fare thee well, Old Joe Clark,
Fare thee well, Old Joe Clark, I say.
Fare thee well, Old Joe Clark, I'm going away."

Will I have to say farewell to my pretty girl? Eric thought, then mentally kicked himself for finding messages even in songs and resolved to enjoy the concert.

Next they did a fast and furious, *Foggy Mountain Breakdown*. The music was heart-thumping, foot-tapping and dance-provoking. Eric wished he had the energy to ask Sherie to dance. He was content to sit, because he was captivated by watching the rapid finger-play of the musicians. Picking or strumming, they worked so fast their fingers blurred.

At the break, Sherie asked, "What do you need?"

Eric fidgeted, annoyed with himself. "I forgot my sketch pad. Can you get me some paper?"

She found a large note pad on Joel's desk and handed it to him. "Do you need a pencil?"

"I always carry a sketching pencil. Thanks."

Eric watched the faces of the performers. They were enjoying each other so much they didn't need an audience. They played for the joy of it, completely engrossed in the music. He wished he could capture the pure pleasure in Joel's face. Cleg demonstrated no signs of self-consciousness when he plucked his tall bass.

Eric dramatized the shine on Snuffy's head in the pencil sketch. He drew quickly, trying to catch the intense concentration on each face.

When Betsy, Russell and Harve arrived, Harve pulled a chair close to Eric. He reached into his backpack and pulled out his sketching pad. He found another one for Eric.

The band switched to a ballad, now with Lou Ann picking her banjo. *Black is the Color of My True Love's Hair.*

"I love the ground whereon she goes ..."

So, there were others who loved as he and Kate did, Eric thought.

Lou Ann's hair – the color of an Irish Setter – fell softly around her face.

"Alone, my life would be so bare ...

I would sigh, I would weep, I would never fall asleep ..."

Eric was grateful when the song was over, Lou Ann shook her hair back and said they were ready for a change of pace. She explained that the next number had its roots just out of Spruce Pine. She began to play and sing *Frankie and Johnny*. All the other players joined in on the refrain, "He was her man, but he done her wrong."

Frankie got even, for according to the song, "that gal could shoot" and she shot him dead.

The music was full of images of rural cabins, craggy mountains, coon dogs and possums, churches and lost love. Eric listened to the Appalachian music, so entirely different than the New York Symphony, and he compared these artists to the tuxedo dressed symphony. Joel's band wore blue jeans and plaid shirts. Eric loved both kinds of music but realized he had missed hearing the music he had grown up on.

They played songs Eric hadn't heard in years. Sometimes the tempo was rapid – notes crashing in to each other – and sending thumping vibrations bouncing back from the walls. Other times, the music was mellow and melodic. Some songs were mournful,

127

expressing the sadness of revenge and death.

Eric asked, "Do you know the Negro spiritual, *Joshua Fought the Battle of Jericho?*" If he was going to hear messages in every song, he was going to pick at least one song.

Joel shook his head. "Any of the rest of you know that song?"

"Sure," Snuffy said. "I haven't seen any music to it, but it goes like this:

"Joshua fit the battle ob Jerico, Jerico, Jerico
Joshua fit de battle ob Jerico
An' de walls come tumblin' down."

Joel began to pick at his guitar. "Try key of G." They began to improvise and in a few minutes, the band had it down. Snuffy sang.

Eric beat time on the arm of the chair, willing the wall between himself and Kate to come down like the one at Jerico.

At the end, Clem pulled a low sounding moan from his bass fiddle, and the group got a little hysterical.

"Wish our drummer was here. He could do a slow drum roll – and then a huge 'crash' on the cymbals when the walls fall down. We don't have many Negro spirituals in our repertoire. We'll have to work on that one, Eric," Joel said.

Joel presented Darlin Scuggs with her violin. She was a tall girl, with long hair and large brown eyes. Just as Eric expected, she started with a ballad. The violin sang as sweetly as a song sparrow. Next, she played, *Seeing Nelly Home*. After she had played the lead through once, Sherie sang, with Darlin playing backup.

"In the sky the bright stars glittered,
On the banks the pale moon shone;
It was from Aunt Dinah's quilting party,
I was seeing Nelly home."

On the final chorus, each band member sang the final "home" in harmony. The song lingered in Eric's mind, like the bay of a coon hound.

"I was seeing Nelly home ...
I was seeing Nelly home."

The harmony seemed to hang in the air and Eric wished they would sing it again. He didn't fight the impulse when his mind substituted "seeing Katy home" for the traditional words.

After *When You and I Were Young, Maggie*, they played a rapid *Wabash Cannonball*, *Grandma's Feather Bed* and finally, an old gospel song, *The Church In The Wildwood.*

Eric didn't want the evening to end, but he was very tired. He stood up and fell back with a crash into the chair as though the cannonball had jumped the track and plowed into his chest. Eric felt embarrassed, but when Betsy offered him her hand, he stood up again. This time he fell back with such force that the recliner skidded back against the wall and he lost consciousness for a few seconds. When he came to, Lou Ann was holding one hand, checking his pulse and Betsy was holding the other and calling his name. Eric heard the panic in her voice.

"We need to get his blood pressure," Lou Ann said, and Sherie shot out of the door to get her blood pressure equipment.

The band members stood mute, watching, their faces taut with concern. Then, finally, they began, slowly, to put their instruments away. Eric heard the sound of zippers and clicks on the catches as they closed the cases.

Harve picked up Eric's sketches from the floor where they had fallen. He compared them to his own and corrected his drawing with a couple of lines.

Sherie announced, worriedly, that his blood pressure was "67 over 40."

"Eric," Lou Ann said, "I'll call Dr. Ross tonight to see if she can check you out tomorrow – that is, unless your family thinks we should call an ambulance tonight." When she saw the concern in Joel and Betsy's faces, she said, "A drop in blood pressure is not too unusual in dialysis patients, but I can't advise you on what to do."

"Check it again in a few minutes, Sherie," Joel suggested and Lou Ann nodded in agreement.

"I'll be all right," Eric protested. He didn't want them to call an ambulance. All he wanted to do was to lie down in his bed.

After his blood pressure had climbed up a few millimeters, band members were reassured and began to leave. "Call us if you need us," each one insisted. Lou Ann and Darlin lingered until the family was back in the house.

Joel said, "Eric, either you call Kate or I will."

"Don't bother her! She's coming tomorrow anyway and I don't want her to be worried on the road. Her brother is bringing her."

In the end, they let him climb the stairs to his room, Joel on one side and his sister on the other. Betsy promised him a large downstairs room in the morning. "Our B&B guests are going home."

"One of us will take you to the clinic tomorrow," Sherie said.

"I suspect I'll be fine by morning. I'll go early to have Dr. Ross check me out."

He would remember the tenderness in his brother's voice. "Leave your door open so we can check on you during the night."

He knew that they would.

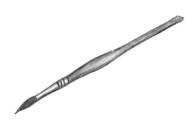

Chapter Nineteen

In the end, they compromised: Eric drove, but Sherie followed him to the clinic. "I have to go to town anyway," she insisted.

Dr. Ross was as reassuring as she could be under the circumstances. She called Dr. Young in New York and, with his approval, made a slight adjustment in Eric's medication.

"I understand that you're on a transplant list," she said. "Good luck. I hope you'll receive good news soon."

When she had installed him in his station, Lou Ann said, "Eric, have you ever given away something that you valued very much?"

He suspected that she was on his case also; trying to influence his decision about taking the gift of life from his son. He hesitated, then decided the best escape was to be flippant. "I gave a pint of blood for Kate's engagement ring."

Lou Ann smiled, but he could see that she was a little disappointed in his answer. "Was the ring pretty?"

"Only if you had a magnifying glass. I promised to replace it when I got a better job, but she still loves that one."

"Just think about it while you are having your blood cleansed," she advised with a slight reproach in her voice.

More meddling people! Eric thought, and reminded himself that he thought the same thing about the pastor's sermon Sunday. Why couldn't people just leave him alone?

He focused his thoughts on Harve and his art work. The boy had talent, no question about it. Eric intended to give Harve the encouragement that no one had given him. Well, that wasn't exactly right. He thought about his grandfather and Miss Leveau. She had given him much encouragement during that first year of high school art. Under her direction he had started a large picture at home.

"I want it to be your most challenging work," she had said. She studied his sketches at intervals and gave him suggestions, but she had not seen the painting. Only Pastor Earl had been invited to look at it and Eric kept it covered when he was not at home. Pastor Earl made Eric blush with his praise.

"God has given you a marvelous talent," Pastor Earl had said.

Eric worked quietly all winter, trying to ignore his father's contempt for his work and complaining about the time Eric spent alone in his room, painting. He planned to enter his work in the first Avery County Art Festival in Newland.

One day he finally took the painting to Miss Leveau.

***

Early that Saturday morning, Eric stripped the mounting tape from the corners and removed his painting from the home-made easel. He patted the edges of the paper, trying to flatten them out. It was stiff from the water wash, but the paper also felt light-weight and flimsy. He cut a piece of cardboard the same size – twenty-four inches by sixteen inches – and slid the watercolor paper onto that. He crept down the stairs and laid it carefully on the back seat of the car.

It was his first full day as a licensed driver and his first permission to drive the car alone. That excitement sustained him emotionally until he parked at the court house where the art work for the competition was to be displayed and judged. He had an hour before the deadline, and he considered driving over to Tony's Drive In for a coke and just skipping the whole thing.

Doubts assailed him and he sat for a few minutes in the car, fidgety and uncertain. Perhaps he should wait until next year to enter. He leaned across the back of the seat to gaze at his painting. Maybe the colors were too vivid, or perhaps they appeared too washed out, especially in the sky. The painting suddenly seemed too "busy" to him. It looked amateurish. He thought of reneging on his promise to Miss Leveau, but he owed her some kindness. Finally, he remembered Pastor Earl's praise and all his lifelong yearning returned. He wanted, so much, to earn respect for his art.

He felt very self-conscious as he carried the painting up the stairs and paused at the desk to register.

"Oh, Eric!"

He turned toward the New England accent and hardly recognized Miss Leveau without her white smock and sneakers. Her little black heels clicked across the marble floor.

Her eyes drank in every detail of the painting. "Oh!" she whispered. "And the title?"

He stammered. "Title? Oh, 'The Master Craftsman'," he blurted.

"*Per-fect!*" She handed him an entrance form. "Eric, do you have a mat?"

He stared at her and he could feel his face getting warm. "A mat?" He felt foolish.

"Never mind. I'll mat it for you."

He thanked her. The hallway was hot and he wanted to get out of the building. "I need to add this note – for my grandmother." He twisted and reached into his back jean pocket and pulled out a little card. He smoothed it and placed it in her hand.

"Based on sketches by Harvey Walsh." She read it aloud. "Your father?"

"My grandad."

"I'll attach your note to the mat. Good luck, Eric." She extended her hand and he took it in his, hoping his sweating palm wouldn't offend her.

He managed a quick look around the hallway to admire the other entries and he slipped quietly away. All the other pictures were framed. He was completely out of his league.

***

Eric left the clinic with a handful of samples and a prescription. He didn't pause to chat with Lou Ann, even when she told him she wanted to meet Kate.

"Are you coming to The Pass Friday night?" she called after him.

"I don't know how long we'll be here."

He was already frustrated when he noticed a police officer in-specting his car. Now what? His throat felt hot with annoyance.

"What's wrong, officer. I am sure I parked okay."

The officer turned his back slightly and began writing in his pad. He muttered something Eric couldn't understand.

"I asked, 'What's wrong?'" He didn't care if his anger was showing.

"Just a citation for past heinous crimes in Avery County."

Now throughly mad, Eric wondered what the fine would be if he took a swing at the officer.

Then, recognition registered and he grabbed the hand of the policeman. "Wyn!"

"Hi, Eric. Gotcha, didn't I?"

"I was about to smack you right in the kisser."

Each man stepped back and studied the other one. Eric was not surprised to see sharp creases in Wyn's blue uniform and an impec-cably neat shirt.

"I called Betsy and she told me you'd be here and might need an escort home. Vi told me you were visiting."

"I don't need an escort, but how about some coffee? Policeman do take breaks, don't they?" Eric could not believe this experience.

As they sat in The Coffee House, eating donuts, catching up on the more than thirty years since they had seen each other, the men pulled out photographs of their families. Wyn said, "This is my Gwen. Can you believe someone that beautiful married me?"

"Nor can I believe my Kate married me!"

"Well, we aren't really so bad – quite fine catches – actually," Wyn boasted and some of the old Wyn came to the surface, to Eric's absolute delight.

"So what are you doing at this clinic?"

"The old man's getting old."

Wyn said, "We both are."

"I'm waiting for a kidney transplant," Eric said.

Wyn wrinkled his forehead, and drew his head back. "You don't say! How come you let yourself get into that shape? A lot of riotous New York living? No, not you. You were the poster boy for good, clean living."

"It just happens. I guess I ran around with the wrong crowd in high school."

"But," Wyn said, "are you on an organ transplant list? Heard it took years sometimes to get one and then it might not be a good organ. Could be diseased or something."

"Thanks for your encouragement. Actually, I am considering accepting a kidney from a live donor. A live donor with the same blood type promises to be much more successful," Eric explained and was grateful that Wyn didn't press him for details.

They made plans to get together with their wives before Eric left the area and when they shook hands Eric said, "I was about ready to slug you for writing me a ticket."

"I know," Wyn said. "I could see it in your eyes."

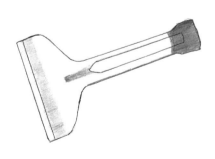

CHAPTER TWENTY

BOTH JOEL AND SHERIE ate in town, so Eric's mother invited him into her apartment for lunch.

"This is nice," he said, looking around the pleasant little apartment. She prepared his favorite sandwiches, sliced apples and peanut butter. He told her about meeting Wyn.

"We lost contact with the family after Homer got a good job in Johnson City. I think he became a police detective. Betsy still sees Vi every once in awhile. How did he look?"

"Like a little Bantam rooster. He was writing a ticket for me when I came out of the clinic!"

Mrs. Walsh laughed. "Well, he always had his supply of inflated ego."

Mother and son were quiet awhile, each enjoying the salad and sandwiches. Then Eric asked, "Mom, are you still praying about –"

"Of course, dear. I am praying that the wall between you will – will just tumble down."

"But what if I make the wrong decision and Clay dies or my body rejects his kidney?"

"That's why we have to walk with faith. No one has any guarantee about tomorrow. It's like driving a mountain road you have never been on. You never know what is around the next boulder, or the next curve."

He sighed. "I haven't lived with faith in a long time."

She didn't preach. She smiled and patted his hand. When he stood up, so did she and they shared an affectionate hug.

***

Eric's mom and his sister had moved his clothes and belongings to the B&B while he was at the clinic. He was delighted with the master bedroom. "It will be like a second honeymoon," he said.

But it was on the far side of the house, and he wanted to be closer to the driveway so he could hear Kate and Lee arrive. So, he waited in the living room of his mom's house. He looked at the recliner, but rejected it. He had had enough of recliners after his four hours at the clinic. He took off his shoes and stretched out on the couch, letting his long legs hang over the arm rest. He had a perfect view of the painting above the fireplace. He had worked diligently on it all that winter. His aim was to paint something his father would think was good enough to hang on the wall, something that could sway his father's attitude about his art. He realized it was an unrealistic goal; something like writing a love letter to someone who had told you to drop dead.

He was caught off guard the day the winners were announced at the first Avery County Art Festival.

***

He had avoided thinking about the competition all day but at supper Betsy announced that she and her grandmother had guessed the subject of his painting.

Eric frowned at her, wondering what she was talking about.

"We think that you painted a picture of your wall – maybe with Soccer in it. We want to call it 'Stonewalling'."

Eric laughed. "My *wall*? Would I spend all winter painting a stupid picture of the wall?"

"You might," his father said unexpectedly, "if you had a lot of pride in it. Grandpa used to draw pictures of all our best work. He'd say, 'Albert, that job is easy on the eyes'."

The phone rang then and Betsy nearly upset the table, splashing iced tea on the tablecloth, getting to it. She hollered from the living room. "Eric, Wyn said you won the competition!"

Eric dropped his fork. His grandmother squealed.

"What'd you say?" he asked, stunned.

She repeated her astounding announcement from the doorway. "Wyn said you won, and to come quickly. They need to take your picture."

Eric started to stand up.

"Just a minute," his father admonished. "Your mother and your grandmother worked hard on this meal. We'll eat supper like civilized people and then ..." He sighed. "We might as well go to the festival – all of us."

Eric picked up his fork and mechanically resumed his meal. He looked at his grandmother. She lowered her head and glanced at him over the rim of her glasses. Then she winked at him.

They walked quietly down the hall, resisting Betsy's plea to hurry. Eric felt embarrassed again that he had not bought a frame for his picture. He wasn't even sure what a mat was.

His heart was beating so hard he was afraid his family could hear it when they approached the winner's circle at the end of the hall. He was a winner! Awesome. He controlled his sudden desire to turn cartwheels down the corridor.

They moved slowly past the honorable mentions and paused at third place, done in pastels. It was a picture of a flower arrangement. Eric could hear Grandma murmuring her approval. The second place entry was of a deer drinking in a mountain stream, and he heard Betsy sigh.

Eric took a deep breath and looked at the first place winning entry. It was a snow scene, and it wasn't his picture.

His heart dropped to his shoes as he realized he had not won the competition. He hadn't won! It was a cruel, horrible trick. *Why*, Wyn?

His throat was folding in on itself and his insides were shriveling. The silence behind him told him that the family was also confused.

He had to run. He turned to escape but stumbled against his father who blocked the way. Eric engaged in a scrimmage to get around him, but his dad held him. He didn't want to look up, but something in the stance of his father, or some need drawing from his pain, caused him to lift his eyes to his father. His dad was staring at something with such intensity that Eric turned slowly around to see.

On a pedestal, elevated above all the other entries was an easel. His picture was there with a banner: Best in Show Award by Eric Walsh.

It was exquisitely matted in a soft gray that accented the color of the stones in his picture and a blue border gave a professional authority to the presentation.

Eric took a deep breath. Then he spun around to study his father's face.

Mr Walsh stood transfixed. "Did you paint that?"

"Yessir." He answered, joining two words into one.

The long silence was unnerving. "Old Ledford place," Mr. Walsh said finally. "Burned down ten years ago."

Albert Walsh stared at a picture of himself, high on a scaffold, adding the final course of stones to a chimney. In the foreground, Eric's grandfather, Harvey, busy at a mud box, paused with a hoe to look up at his son.

"You couldn't have known all these details." He said, astonished.

Was his dad accusing him of cheating? Numb with hurt, Eric just pointed to his note on the mat.

His father leaned close to the picture and read out loud. "Based on sketches –" his lips quivered, but he continued in a husky voice. "– by Harvey Walsh."

Albert Walsh nodded. Quietly he said, "It's easy on the eyes, boy. Mighty easy on the eyes."

Eric gulped. There was a stinging in the back of his eyes. He brushed his sweaty hands along the sides of the legs of his pants and asked, "Would Grandpa like it?"

"Son, I reckon he would be turning cartwheels all the way down this hallway!"

The next few minutes were blurred in Eric's memory. Flashes from cameras burning his eyes; Wyn lugging in a large tripod and heavy camera; his grandmother's tears as she caressed the note; the fancy reception; and Miss Leveau introducing him to a rotund man with a round, red face.

"Eric," Miss Leveau said, "This is Mr. Harry Woodwright, from the governor's office in Raleigh. He served as one of our judges and he wants to talk to you."

Eric glanced entreatingly at his dad and Mr. Walsh came to stand beside him. Miss Leneau introduced the two men.

Mr. Woodwright bowed from the waist, like a television English butler. "We are collecting paintings for a new display at the governor's mansion in Raleigh. I think yours is outstanding, although we do not usually acquire watercolors – not that they are inferior, but they take special care since they need to be covered in glass. We would like for you to loan us *The Master Craftsman*."

Eric could hardly speak. "But," he whispered, "I am giving the painting to my father."

"It's not for sale." Mr. Walsh said.

"It so eloquently expresses an important aspect of our mountain heritage. We could make a copy for you," Mr. Woodwright said with quiet formality.

"The picture is not for sale." Eric's dad said again.

"We are only asking for a loan, at this time. We can have it reproduced for you, the same colors and the same size. The painting will be a part of a prestigious new North Carolina exhibition. Of course we could negotiate a sale later."

Mr. Walsh cleared his throat. "There isn't enough money in the world to buy it. That's my father, you see." He pointed to the older man in the picture. "And the picture was painted by my son."

Grandma had risen from her seat and she came to stand with them. She laid her hand gently on her son's arm. "Son, he asked for a *loan* of the picture. And Albert, your father always wanted to visit the governor's mansion."

Mr. Walsh chuckled. He looked at Eric and Eric nodded. "How soon will we get a copy of it?"

"Right away, sir, and thank you." He shook Mr. Walsh's hand. He bowed to Eric's grandmother and he bowed to Eric. "Amazing craftsmanship," he said, backing away from them. "Extraordinary."

Chapter Twenty-One

Eric lay on the couch for several minutes, then sat up, uncomfortable and restless. Leaning his left shoulder against the back, he could at least stretch out his legs. He and Kate had an "extended" size sofa in their living room in New York.

His father's pride in his painting had given Eric incredible joy. He reached behind him for the pillow. It was as lumpy and uncomfortable as the thoughts that swirled around inside his brain. He stood up to fluff up the pillow and added another he found on a chair. He tried to shake it up also but it was more firmly packed and wouldn't "fluff." I should've gotten a pillow from the bed, he thought. Oh, Kate, what can I tell you? I'm almost as confused as I was when we left home.

He checked his watch. If they left Lexington by nine, they could be here any minute. But knowing Kate, it was unlikely that they had left so early. Would she still be angry with him?

"You should not be so selfish," she had said one night. "At least consider me. I don't want to be a widow."

Eric winched. She would grieve for him, he knew. He walked around the room, gazing at the art hanging on the walls. Some were very good – done after he finished art school. One or two were excellent. Then, he returned to the one hanging over the fireplace. While it was hanging at the governor's mansion, the state had covered it with a special glass that didn't reflect the light and his parents had left it that way. He would have to ask his mom if she still had the print. He wanted it for his office in New York.

141

Eric considered his painting at length. Some aspects could be improved, now that he understood the principles of art. But the image of his grandfather surprised him, it was so well done. The old man almost spoke to him. "Hi, Grandpa," Eric spoke aloud in the empty room. "I might be joining you sooner than we expected."

It was amazing that years after his death, Eric had been able to recall and paint every feature of his grandfather. He wasn't sure he could do that for his father now, but he had been very much alive when Eric painted this picture. His eyes rested on the image of his father and a lump formed in his throat. *We didn't always agree, but I respected and loved you, Dad. I just couldn't please you with my career choice – and that hurt.*

His dad had been surprised; no, he was astounded when he first saw the painting. Eric guessed he was expecting some crayon-type picture because he hadn't bothered to look at his work in a long time.

"Easy on the eyes," his father had said, and it was just about the highest compliment he could pay.

Dad, Eric thought, looking at the man in his picture, *I guess I never understood your love, nor was aware of the depth of it.* His father cared enough for him to carry a photo of him in his wallet, as Durrell told him.

Back aching, Eric moved to the recliner and after playing around with the unfamiliar lever on the side of the chair a minute, he figured out how to work it. He pulled back on the lever, raised his legs and leaned back, but he couldn't relax. He looked again at the picture. It was well named. All of them were master craftsmen – his grandfather, his father, and the artist who painted it.

His thoughts drifted back to the clinic and Lou Ann.

"Eric," she had asked, "have you ever given away something that you valued very much?"

He could think of nothing that he had ever given away that could compare to the offering and *acceptance* of his painting, *The Master Craftsman*. What would he have done had his father rejected it, or had simply acknowledged it as though it were a third place ribbon from a foot race in the school's track meet?

Eric had felt affirmed – validated – by his father's pleasure. *A painting.*

In comparison, he was rejecting part of Clay's living body. What would his son feel if *his father* rejected his gift of life?

He thought his father was obstinate and bullheaded – but wasn't he behaving the same way? He had never looked at the situations from Clay's viewpoint.

Remembering his talk with Kathy, Eric thought, I guess that when you think you are self sacrificing for your family, you may be placing your family in jeopardy because they need you.

Eric pushed the lever on the recliner, lowering his legs, and sat up straight. He covered his face with his hands. What if Clay died? That was his fear. "Greater love has no man than this, that a man lay down his life for his friend." It didn't make it any easier that this situation included a possibility, however remote, of a son laying down his life for a father.

Why hadn't Jesus explained the etiquette about *accepting*? It is far more complicated than it sounds. He said it was more blessed to give than to receive. In this case, it was *a lot easier* to give than to receive. He would rather be on the giving end.

God, what can I do? He was totally helpless. He couldn't make a decision. His mother said he had to walk in faith, but how did he do that? "We must pray," she said.

Why am I put in a position that I have to *take*? Power comes in *giving*. But, he wasn't concerned about *power*. It was either life or death.

Then, he thought of the pastor's sermon last Sunday in the little mountain church. Pete Sands told of his facing death while he was traveling in his kayak. "I finally realized that I was going to drown – unless I asked God to save me." Eric sat still, weighing the idea in his mind. It was just as true for him as it had been for the pastor.

Suddenly, he wanted to get on his knees and beg for help. He realized that he was too weak to do it, so Eric sat upright in the recliner and cried for help. He, too, was at the absolute end of his rope, just as Pete Sands had described his exhaustion and feeling of defeat.

"God, help me figure this out," Eric heard his grandfather say one day when one of his uncles had asked for advice about how to handle a problem.

"God, I haven't talked with you much lately," Eric began. It was like checking in with a beloved relative by long distance. "But I need you now." Eric tried the same words his grandfather used, whispering them aloud, "God, help me figure this out." To his amazement, he found that his face was flooded with tears.

How long did he sit, praying? He hadn't thought of it as praying; he was simply asking for directions.

"God, tell me what I should do." He took a deep breath and waited. He didn't get an answer immediately, but he began to feel a peace, a surrender to the Deity. He had begged for help from the God of his father and his grandpa – and he sincerely expected an answer. Joy filled his heart and seemed to spread over his entire body. He felt contentment that he had not known in a long, long time and he knew that it was not just because Kate was coming. He was not sure yet what God would tell him to do, but he felt a serenity that he would make the right decision.

"Thank you, God," he whispered. He yielded his life to the master of the land and sea. He leaned back and slowly pulled the lever back, elevating his feet. It was as though his kayak had landed safely on the island shore.

Eric dozed. He was awakened by the sound of Princess barking and a car horn announcing the arrival of Kate and Lee.

He shoved the chair lever so he could sit up and almost leaped from the recliner. He hurried to the door. He watched as his mom and Princess welcomed his Kate. He hadn't realized his mother had been waiting on the front porch.

Sherie ran to the car, and Joel arrived from his studio. Betsy hurried across the lawn from the B&B, where she had been preparing the bedroom for them.

Eric stood in the doorway and watched. His Kate. Sherie opened the door and she stepped out of the car like a queen. She hugged his mother, then pushed her away to look at her and then pulled her close to her heart again. She did the same to Sherie, Joel and Betsy. Ever gracious, revealing her gentle, caring concern for each of them. She was wearing an ankle-length full skirt just as she had when he first saw her. Her sleeveless blouse showed off her long, slender arms. Her brown hair draped gracefully around her face and shoulders.

He watched her pick up Princess as the family welcomed her brother, Lee. Eric's heart was beating furiously as he stepped out a few steps on the porch, still holding the screen door ajar. She turned to look at him. His breath caught. Their eyes locked and held a moment and it was as though there had never been a quarrel between them. He let the screen door slam.

Kate handed Princess back to his mother, and, without taking her eyes from his, left the others to run across the lawn and up the steps to his waiting arms.

Chapter Twenty-Two

BEFORE AN ELABORATE welcome dinner Mom and Sherie had prepared for Kate, Eric asked Lee to walk with him to see his "project." Lee was tall – slightly over six feet and muscular. Eric envied his physique. Ten years younger than Kate, he had followed his father's career and became a fine horseman. With a little help from Kate and Eric, he had rebuilt the stables and turned the family farm back into a thriving business.

"Thanks for bringing Kate, Lee."

"It was my pleasure, but I couldn't drive fast enough for her . I could have let Chuck bring her but I wanted to see you. Can you believe that my son is old enough for a driver's license?"

"We never believe our children have grown up. Has Kate told you what Clay wants to do?"

"Yes, and I admire him tremendously. You must be very proud of him."

"Lee, if you were in my place, would you –?"

"I don't know, Eric. You must be terribly important to him! I wish I could have donated an organ to my father."

They sat in the rocking chairs on the porch, following dinner. Lee said, "What an indescribable beautiful setting. Wonderful scenery, great food and fun fellowship. I just wish I could have heard your band play, Joel. Kate sends me all your CDs."

Joel answered, "Well, thank you, kind sir. We are giving a concert at The Pass Friday night. Better stay over."

"Wish I could! I have to get back tomorrow. I've been trying to decide what makes your band so superior to others I have heard."

"I don't know which bands you have heard," Joel said, "but I can tell you this. Each musician I take on is a gifted musician. Some have been playing for forty years. We love each other, we love playing together and we love the music."

Eric said, "You and Kate should have heard them last night! You wouldn't believe it."

Kate asked, "Is that what made you pass out?"

"Who told you that?" Eric looked at his brother.

"I told you that I would tell her if you didn't. However, Eric, I didn't tell her until she was safely here."

"I was going to tell her. I'll see my doctor next week because we're catching a plane in Johnson City early Sunday morning. Not much can happen before then."

They sat silently for a few minutes, each rocking at his own rhythm, and thoughts. Eric guessed he should have been angry

147

with Joel, but he wasn't. He and Sherie had shown him nothing but love all week.

Joel continued talking about his favorite subject. "I have been fascinated by mountain music all my life – the music and the instruments. Some of the instruments seem primitive. I have friends who can poke a stick into the bottom of a tub, attach some strings and produce an instrument. In fact, we will have Ole Tommy playing his tub Friday night. The banjos were easily made in the mountains – some of the first ones were made out of gourds. The pioneers made softer-sounding banjos by using groundhog hide or bobcat skin for the head. Some of the earlier craftsmen turned out fine fiddles and guitars." Joel was as passionate about his music as Eric was about his art.

Sherie spoke up. "Speaking of instruments, we have a surprise. We have to perform before it gets dark." She had been sitting at the end, chatting with Lee.

Eric's mom said, "Kate would you mind holding Princess for a moment?"

Kate answered, "You sound mysterious."

Sherie retrieved two elongated hour-glass shaped string instruments from the table at the end of the porch. "Dulcimers," she explained, as she showed one to Kate and gave the other to Mrs. Walsh. "Grandma called them 'dulcymore,' and the name means 'sweet tone'," she said. "Some claim that they are the instruments of the angels."

"Teaching me has been quite a chore, for Sherie, I'll tell you," Mrs. Walsh said, laughing. She placed the wood instrument flat on her knees and reached into her blouse pocket for a pick.

"Mom, you have music in the soul."

"Wish it'd show up in my fingers. What did you tell me, Sherie – an idiot can learn to play a dulcimer in three minutes, but it took you five minutes to learn?"

Joel said, "They asked me to write a homecoming song for you, Kate, but I didn't get around to it."

"So," Mrs. Walsh said, "now you will have to settle for *The Little Brown Jug.*

"Okay by me," Lee said and everyone laughed.

"I guess that's better than *Whiskey before Breakfast*, Sherie said. Then seeing their perplexed expressions she explained: "That's the name of another of our songs, but see if you remember this one." She played a chord and both ladies began playing the old folk song, strumming lightly with their picks on the four-string instruments.

Eric moved his chair beside Kate to watch his mother just as Sherie began to sing,

"My wife and I live all alone
In a little hut we call our own.
She loves gin and I love rum,
I can tell you , we have fun'."

They paused for Sherie to tell them the words to the chorus so they could all join in.

"Ha ha ha, you and me,
Little Brown Jug, how I love thee."

"You all sing!" Mrs. Walsh entreated and no one wanted to disappoint her. They sang, fumbling with the words at first, and growing in confidence, the six got into the spirit of the song and belted out the words. "Ha ha ha – " And Princess began to bark.

Happy laughter rippled around the porch.

Eric had been familiar with the dulcimer from his childhood. He could close his eyes and draw them, but tonight they looked and sounded different. They were *different* from the instruments he had learned to love in New York. The music sounded like a whisper in comparison to a guitar twang, but it had a soft, plaintive sound, perfect for evening entertainment on a mountain home porch.

Lee said, "Those produce a sound that isn't full bodied, but it surely is sweet. Excuse me, Mrs. Walsh and Sherie. I don't mean that it isn't as lovely as the guitar. I don't know the musical terms to describe it"

Joel said, "That's okay, Lee. The rest of us grew up with dulcimers and guitars."

Mrs. Walsh said, "I know *Skip To My Lou*." Eric watched his mother carefully place her fingers on the fingerboard, using her pointer and ring finger. She began to strum. "Come on, Sherie

– don't hang me out to dry!"

Eric leaned back to watch his mother, his pride growing for her with each song.

Sherie joined her and after they had played a stanza or two, she gave the others the words.

"Lost my partner, what'll I do?
Lost my partner, what'll I do?
Skip to my Lou my darlin."

After the first peppy lines were repeated, the sextet began to sing and the song ended in wild laughter. "We sing like a bunch of drunken hillbillies," Kate said and Eric responded. "I don't know about 'drunk' but we *are* hillbillies, and I use the term proudly."

"Where did this instrument come from?" Kate asked Sherie. She reached over to touch the dulcimer.

Sherie explained, "I know the banjo was a favorite folk instrument brought to America by the slaves from Africa and Jamaica but no one, that I know, can tell me where the dulcimers came from. One old timer gave me the best answer. He said, 'They have always been in Appalachia'."

"The dulcimer is one of our oldest instruments," Joel explained. "It is one that the rural people could make themselves – just as they could the banjo and other simple instruments."

"What is that one made from, Sherie?"

"This one is wormy chestnut on the top and cherry on the bottom. Mom's has butternut on the top and another hardwood – probably walnut – on the bottom. They found that a softer wood works better on the top, with a hardwood bottom."

"Does different wood affect the tone of the instrument?" Kate wanted to know.

Sherie turned to Joel. "What do you think?"

"I think it does, somewhat. Some of the dulcimers have a 'false bottom', a second layer of wood, placed on spacers. That increases volume. It keeps player's legs from absorbing the sound. Play another folk song."

Mrs. Walsh offered her instrument to her daughter-in-law.

"Don't you want to try, Kate?"

"Not tonight, I'm afraid. But, could you teach me while we're here? This gives me an idea for a great book."

"I know you're tired, dear, and it's almost too dark to see. Let's do just one more, Sherie."

"How about *Shenandoah*?" She began to play and sing about longing to hear the rolling river. It was played slower and was making each of the listeners sleepy. Many of the old songs were somber, perhaps reflecting the hardships and loneliness of the early Appalachian people. Music provided much of the social life. At neighborhood gatherings, everybody brought his instruments."

Sherie said, "But for a long time, women were not allowed to play the instruments. They were only allowed to sing."

When they were through with *Shenandoah*, Kate and Eric started across the lawn to the B&B and to their room. Lee went to the car for his bag. "I'm leaving early, Sis. Don't get up."

"Of course I will. I'll fix you coffee before you leave."

Joel told her, "The coffee pot is ready and the timer will turn it on at five."

Eric laughed. "There's something good to say about a few things in the modern age."

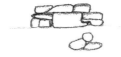

Chapter Twenty-Three

They hurried across the driveway and up the sidewalk to the B&B like two excited teenagers. "First, I'd like a quick walk through of the downstairs," Kate said.

"Why not? We *are* half owners, you know." Eric whispered in her ear.

"It's so beautifully done, and larger than I expected. The decorator surely admires some artist by the name of Eric Walsh. His pictures are in every room. There are one or two that I haven't seen before tonight." She turned toward him with uncertainty written across her brow. "We should have insisted that Lee stay here."

Eric laughed. "I think they wanted us to be alone."

"Great idea," Kate said, and walked into his inviting arms.

Later, they lay together in the big bed and Kate said, "Sweetheart, I sense something different. You seem ... relaxed? No. Peaceful. You don't seem as resigned as you used to."

"I'm not resigned to the idea of dying at all. I want to live to share life with you for many more years. I have had a wonderful spiritual experience, Kate. It would be hard to explain and you might laugh, although we used to be regular in our church worship," Eric said.

"Try me. Please, just tell me." Her large eyes looked wide with concern as she studied him.

"I went to church with Mom and the young preacher really reached me." He told her about Pete Sand's experience in the kayak in the Pamlico Sound. "He would have died had he not just yielded to the waves, and let God take over." He paused and she seemed to sense the importance of what he had to say. He felt, suddenly, self-conscious. "I asked God to show me the way."

Kate put her arm across his chest and laid her cheek against him. "I don't know why, but I always thought that when you were sure of what you needed to do, it might be a spiritual decision. I have never quit praying, Eric."

He could feel her tears on his chest and he remembered his own tears shortly before she arrived. "I don't know what will happen, but I'm at peace with my life. I don't know my final decision but I feel confident that it will be the right one. But, Kate, you must face the possibility that nothing will work. In spite of everything, I could die. My body could reject any transplant. Have you realized how lucky I am to have renal disease? There are some replaceable parts. Incredible! Cancer patients and some other seriously ill people do not have that option!"

She sat up to stare down at him. "I remember Dr. Young saying something like that when you were first diagnosed. He said your swollen legs and feet could be evidence of heart disease and other things, but the best diagnosis would be kidney failure. I thought he was nuts, when he said that, but then he added, 'You may later have the option of a kidney transplant'."

He smiled and wrapped a strand of her long hair around his finger. "And you begged to be tested right then. Thank you, Sweetheart. Even though you were not a match, I saw your love."

"I keep thinking that if you were not on the transplant lists, it would mean that there could be a kidney for someone else who doesn't have a son like Clay. Also," She leaned down to kiss him. "I worry about what it would do to Clay if you rejected his offer."

"When you kiss me like that, it should seal the bargain – but, I want one last check of the lists. If there is a match, I would feel certain God was providing it."

"Do you remember the exhausting procedure we will have to go through to get on another list? Do you remember all the hoops we have to jump through every day to stay on a list? Are you really willing to go through all those tests again? Our cell phone has become an umbilical chord and it will get worse if you are on other lists."

"Sweetheart, I need you to promise that you'll let the final decision be mine, and I don't want to quarrel about it."

She smiled and nodded, tears running down her face. She wiped her nose with the side of her hand just as he reached for the tissue box on the night stand. She smiled. "You know me pretty well, Eric!"

He waited, watching her pat at her cheeks, before he asked, "What do you want to do tomorrow?"

"I'd like for us to take Mom and anyone else who wants to go for a drive up the Blue Ridge Parkway to Blowing Rock for lunch."

"We'll just want a light lunch. Remember that Betsy is preparing dinner for us tomorrow night."

Just before they turned out the lights, Kate said, "When we retire, we could buy Betsy's part of this house and move down here."

"Let's just rent it for a couple of months each summer. We could bring our grandkids down. Are you ready to retire?"

"No. I'm not, but – "

"I'm not ready either. I have at least six more projects that I want to work on," he said. "And Kathy has talked to me about a position."

"A position? At a veterinary clinic?"

"No. This position is full time. She wants me to be a grandfather to her daughter."

"I didn't know you'd been talking with her."

"We've talked several times. I know the baby's name. Erica. What a shame to brand a kid like that!"

Ever the lover, Kate said, "It's a wonderful name, and a wonderful brand." She snuggled closer to him. "Do you know the other name?" She laughed. "Katherine. Erica Katherine. You're not the only one who's special."

They agreed that they could not leave their children in New York to retire so far away from them yet. Finally, they went to sleep as though each had a guarantee of long, useful lives. Both of them.

Eric woke up with Kate's back snuggled against his – warm and soft. When he stirred and turned to his side; she rolled right into his arms. He caressed her soft, brown hair. He was so glad she had rejected the style craze and never cut her hair too short. "Long hair makes an older woman look older," she had told him. But he loved her long hair – loved every strand of silver that was beginning to peak through the chestnut.

He leaned on his elbow and examined her face. She opened her eyes and he said, "I love the little laugh lines around your eyes."

"You love my wrinkles?"

"I love everything about you. These are character lines, and they remind me that we have had more than thirty years together." He kissed them and she giggled.

On each anniversary they toasted to an equal amount of time in the future. He wanted another thirty years with her!

She slipped out of bed. "I want to see Lee before he leaves," she said and he wanted to thank his brother-in-law for bringing her. They hurriedly dressed and walked across the driveway.

***

They entered the parkway at Spruce Pine, and Kate wanted to stop at every overlook. They marveled again at the many distant peaks and the graduating hues of lavender and blue in the mountains and valleys. "The color changes with the time of the day," Sherie said. She had insisted on driving her SUV and directed Kate to the front seat with her. Eric was content to sit in the back seat with his mother. He wasn't too keen to drive today.

Eric felt lethargic this morning and had difficulty climbing out of the vehicle each time they stopped. Finally, he sat and waited as Kate went ballistic over the scenery. She took dozens of photographs although they had a huge album of similar pictures.

As the SUV climbed toward Linville, Eric thought about his many hikes on the "backside" of Grandfather Mountain – and also of his Boy Scout camping trips down into Globe Valley, on the lower side of the mountain. He had always planned to bring Kathy and Clay for a camping trip in Globe Valley.

155

Kate reacted to the scenery as though she had never seen it before. "We must come back some fall," she said. "The Appalachian's fall leaves are even prettier than those in New England."

The weather was glorious, but there was a promise of rain in the afternoon. Puffy, round cumulus clouds, white with shades of gray and blue accented the skyline. Eric said to himself that if he painted the scene, he would add a touch of pink and purple to the clouds to contrast with the gray.

The women – his mother, his wife and his sister-in-law – each of them a Mrs. Walsh, stood together to listen to the wind in the pine tops. "They're singing," Kate said. "The smell is wonderful. I keep a pine-scented candle on our dining room table, but it isn't the same."

Sherie pointed to the ravens and once she spotted a Peregrine Falcon. She stopped near the Linville exit to show them a flock of wild turkeys. "Both falcons and turkeys were once on the endangered list, but they are both making a dramatic comeback."

"I have lost count of the brilliant red cardinals I have snapped pictures of. I hope we see some deer," Kate said.

"Probably more likely at the upper end of our drive. There are more meadows and pasture lands. But, look at that grouse!" Sherie said. They had to slow down to let the big gray bird saunter arrogantly across the road as though she owned the parkway.

Kate said, "The grouse reminds me of some of the 'summer people' I've seen. They are oblivious to anyone else."

Eric had sketches in his files from every view point, so he sketched lazily today. It would seem odd to his family if he was not sketching and he didn't want to distress them.

As they approached the Blue Ridge Parkway's Linn Cove Viaduct, Kate leaned back in her seat and clutched the arm rests. The viaduct seemed to swerve away from the side of the mountain, like a huge roller coaster.

"Yeow!" Kate suppressed a scream and ducked her head..

For a second time on his trip, Eric was riding in a vehicle that seemed to be jet propelled straight into the sky. He reassured Kate. "The viaduct is a marvel of safety, level, banked just enough and very safe. It's the flatlander in you that makes you afraid.. We'll not die on it."

Dying is the easiest part about living, Eric thought and was stunned at the paradox of this idea. Facing death was no big deal, partly because you had little control over it.. One doesn't choose the time of death, usually. He could almost wish they would just coast painlessly off into the sky and heaven, relieving him of the decision he had to make. However, today, he felt no regret that the SUV sailed smoothly around the curve, seemingly to skim the side of the mountain.

He had an earlier impulse to plunge into the darkness of a mountain canyon on his way up the mountain, that first night after he had rented a car in Johnson City. Since he had prayed about his problem, however, he felt an unaccountable peace that dazzled him. *Dazzled?* Yes, dazzled was not too strong a word. Why had he endured the burden alone so long? Man needed God – especially when he was facing death. He would like to talk with Pete Sands again and he might call him when they got back to his mom's house.

They lunched at the Dew Drop Inn, a small restaurant that seemed to hug the mountains and it gave them a spectacular view of the cliff face called "The Blowing Rock" and the mountains around it. He smiled and patted his mother's hand. She nodded toward the other two and winked. Sherie and Kate continued their rapid fire discussion about the *flora* and *fauna.* Eric and his mother were happy to listen.

However, several times Kate paused to look at Eric. "Are you all right?"

Chapter Twenty-Four

Before they left for his sister's home, Eric asked Kate to check the front closet to see if his grandpa's cane was still stored in it. "It might be one of those extending canes that I can make long enough for me to use."

Kate couldn't find a cane. "You'll have to lean on me, honey."

"And I would hurt your back. I'll be all right."

"Do you want a wheelchair?"

"Of course not!" He spoke too sharply and he saw the hurt in her eyes. "I don't mean to be such a grouch."

"It's okay, Sweetheart. I guess I would feel the same way. We ought to buy you a cane before we start home."

***

Betsy greeted them at the door, before they could even ring the bell. "Everyone's in the kitchen," she said as she ushered them inside. "Hey, you look pretty good for someone who spent the day trekking the Parkway."

"I feel pretty good," Eric said, realizing it was true. He had dozed all the way back from Blowing Rock as the "Missus Walshes" had continued their animated conversation.

Soft light illuminated the entry hall and living room, which featured one of Eric's larger paintings. He had painted it for them as a wedding gift. It was a wood scene, featuring a red fox and her two cubs and next to it was an exquisite carving of a fox. Eric's brother-in-law was a fine woodcarver. He thought, *Perhaps he can*

158

carve me a cane.

Russell and Betsy had bought an old Victorian style house and restored it. Betsy had an uncanny gift and she could turn anything into an attractive home – but she had outdone herself on this one. In the dining room Russell had erected a large showcase for all the sports trophies the boys had won.

Betsy's oldest son, Al, had invited his girlfriend, Jeanne. She seemed tiny enough to fit in Eric's coat pocket and as pretty as she could be. A natural blond, she had a fragile look and it surprised him that she was an excellent skier and was on the kayak team at Lees McCrae College.

"Jeanne wants to write children's books," Betsy explained. "We wanted her to meet Kate."

The beautifully crafted table could seat twelve comfortably and Betsy had used her grandmother's finest china and silverware to set the table. She had made a centerpiece of tiger lilies.

Attractive name cards invited each person to a place reserved for them. Eric's name card had an ink drawing of a giraffe on it; and Kate's had a gazelle, obviously Harve's work. Betsy had placed her boys, Al, Ed, Rusty and Harve among the guests and each son took it as a personal responsibility to be attentive to the guests he was seated with. Harve was on Eric's right and he knew exactly when to refill his water glass or to remove a soup bowl. Al was on one side of their grandmother and Rusty on the other, and they gave her lots of loving attention. No one felt neglected and, once again, Eric had to brag on the training Betsy and Russell had given their sons.

Eric felt a warm glow when Russell asked the blessing and included him and Kate. "Give Eric and Kate a safe trip home, and God, please meet their every need."

Eric was not hungry, but knew he had to eat some of the chicken and dumplings Betsy had prepared because it had always been his favorite meal. He was seldom hungry. He knew, however, he would be hungry for this fellowship once they returned to New York.

Eric felt a growing affection for Betsy's husband, especially seeing how happy he had made her. Bet's first husband was a cad and had abandoned her with one small child and another on the way. Eric and Kate had two children and were saving to buy a home at the time, so were unable to help much. But what little cash they could send was put quietly into Bet's checking account by their parents without her knowing where it had come from.

Jeanne was sitting next to Kate and they were engaged in serious conversation. Eric watched Kate's animated hand gestures. He guessed she was talking with Jeanne about writing. He watched his wife and was filled with love. "Lean on me," she had said, knowing it would hurt her back. Eric had always told his kids that if anything ever happened to him he would want Kate to remarry – but now the thought saddened him. For her to be loved by another man? He would just have to see that nothing happened to him. Then, he noticed that everyone had grown extremely quiet.

Joel spoke, "Eric, Sherie and I need to go to New York soon, and we want to take you home. You would be so much more comfortable in the SUV."

"But, your concert – and I have to return the car to Johnson City."

"We can take care of the car, Uncle Eric," Grant said.

"We can leave immediately after the Friday night concert. It takes us hours to wind down after a concert, and we could take turns driving. We want to do this, Little Brother," Joel said.

Kate replied, "I think it is a generous, thoughtful thing to do – and you haven't been to see us since we landscaped the yard and Eric built the outdoor barbecue and fireplace."

Eric had trouble swallowing. He had not realized how he dreaded the trip home, with long lines and waits at the airports. "Thanks, *Little Brother*. Now if Russell can fix me up with a cane that is long enough for Abraham Lincoln, I'll be fine."

"That can be done," Russell said and excused himself from table.

Jeanne asked, "How can you both be the little brother?"

Eric explained, "He is older than I am and far more distinguished looking, because of his gray hair, but I am taller than he is."

Russell reappeared with two canes. One had an eagle on it, the other the face of an old man. "I haven't cut either of these for size. Which do you like best?"

Eric stood up. It was hard to choose; both were works of art. "I'll take the old man. He looks like me – if I grew a beard."

Russell took the measurement and said, "Canes are one of my best sellers at craft shows. I'll cut it after dinner."

Jeanne then turned to a more serious subject. "Mr. Walsh, I have a cousin who is about to begin dialysis. I don't understand anything about it."

"Do you know which kind your cousin is choosing?"

"I didn't know there was more than one kind," Jeanne said.

"There are two types – hemodialysis and peritoneal dialysis – which offers a manual therapy or a machine driven therapy."

Al suggested that Eric could explain the difference.

Eric was a bit embarrassed. "It is not exactly dinner conversation material."

Betsy reassured him. "We all want to know."

Eric laid down his fork. "In both of the types, the blood is cleansed of waste, extra chemicals and fluid. The hemodialysis is the system I use. I am not exactly sure why I chose that kind, except that there is a clinic only a few blocks from our home. In this dialysis, an artificial kidney is used. Your blood circulates through a hemodialyzer. In the peritoneal dialysis, the peritoneal cavity is slowly filled with dialysate through a catheter. Extra fluid and waste products are drawn out of your blood and into the dialysate bag and then thrown away."

During the conversation, both the younger boys pulled out their wallets. Harve said, "I don't have my driver's license yet, but we each carry a donor's card. In case anything ever happens to Rusty or me, we want our organs to be donated."

Al said, "Actually, we all carry the cards. Mom wouldn't hear of anything else."

"That's wonderful, boys!" Kate said. "Our children do also. Just remember that it is vitally important that your parents know your wishes. They have the authority to cancel your decision if they want to."

Betsy was emphatic. "Do you think we would do that when my own brother is waiting for a kidney donor? And why don't more parents encourage this? They could make something good come from an untimely death."

"Maybe," Kate said. "They just don't want to think about the possibility." Everyone nodded, each with his own thoughts.

"Uncle Eric," Al said, "Last year my roommate at ASU wrote a paper on the Falun Gong scandal in China, but he also wrote about availability of organs in the Far East –"

Russell squared his shoulders, leaned across the table and raised his hand to stop Al. "A gruesome and horrible story. Don't spoil our dinner, son."

"But, I only meant –"

"I don't care what you meant, Al." Russell's voice was not scolding, but it had an authority that hushed Al.

A questioning look crossed Al's face, but as he looked at Eric, he frowned and said quietly, "It was a stupid interruption. Forgive me, Uncle Eric."

Eric had been studying his plate. He said quietly, "It's okay, Al. We have investigated every possibility." He raised his chin and his gaze turned to his brother-in-law. "I know the story, Russell, and there are many more like it. There are lots of grizzly reports, and also some pleas from desperate men who want to *sell* one of their own kidneys. It's simply–" He sighed and seemed hesitant to explain. "I will accept an organ from the national list – but I could never risk the life of another man's son."

Russell nodded and his eyes swept around the table to his four sons.

Jeanne spoke in a soft voice. "I want to donate one of my kidneys to my cousin and I seem to be a fairly good match. What is the operation like?"

Kate said, "I have studied the technique carefully, Jeanne. There have been so many advances in medicine that a perfect match is not necessary now except in unusual cases, like Eric's. He has O negative blood, and that requires a better match. Actually, the laparoscopic surgery requires only a few small incisions, the longest one only about three inches, just big enough to get the kidney out and the patient is in the hospital for less than a week. I really admire you, Jeanne." She leaned around Jeanne to tell Al, "You had better not let this one get away!"

"I don't intend to," Al said and Jeanne blushed.

Kate continued, "Unless one has experienced it, no one can know what it is like for the family of a patient who is waiting for a donor. Every day you wake up, wondering if this will be the day that your loved one will receive a chance to live. You wonder if it will be too late." She paused. "You live with agony every day as you watch someone you love die."

"Yes," said Eric's mother, who talked at a dinner party so infrequently, that everyone turned toward her, "and you realize that, usually, someone will have to die before a kidney can be available. The family of a donor has to give approval for the transplant when they are dealing with the heartbreak of losing one they loved dearly."

Betsy said, "And they have to make the decision at perhaps the lowest ebb of their lives. I admire the families of donors so much. That's why I am so proud of our sons. They made the decision for us. We would just have to honor their wishes."

"I hope you never have to," Eric said quietly.

Everyone was busy with their own thoughts, until Russell asked, "What do you think of Joel's group of musicians?"

"I'm really impressed, but don't any of you boys have musical talent?"

"Al used to play the guitar with us, but he got too busy with school. He still plays with us every once in awhile." Joel leaned across the table to ask, "What are you doing Friday night?"

"I was going to your concert."

"Come play with us in the concert."

Al said, "This is really a great night for me. You all brag on my girlfriend and Uncle Joel asks me to play with his band again."

People had finished their main course and, as Betsy stood up, so did three of her boys. They began to clear the table and take orders for coffee. Kate could not conceal her surprise.

Russell explained, "We have taught them to be extremely fine butlers. Al is excused tonight so he can take care of Jeanne. We cook meals for their friends and they help us with dinner parties and smaller groups of our friends. It's a fair trade."

Eric's mother said, "I wish all our grandchildren lived closer."

Joel said, "We ought to plan a family reunion. Yes, a big one with all the children and grandchildren and great grandchildren. We'll do it next year to celebrate Eric's surgery and your 85th birthday, Mom!"

"I think that is a marvelous idea!" Kate said and they all agreed to make the plans.

"I can tell you that this trip home has meant everything to me. Thank you for everything."

"Don't get all mushy," Rusty teased. "You'll be back next year."

I wonder if I will, Eric thought.

"After the dessert, Uncle Eric," Harve said, "Can you come up to my room to see some of my work?"

"Why isn't some of your work on the walls down here?"

"Because," Betsy said, "he won't let me hang any of his pictures. He says he's embarrassed to display his work beside yours."

"Nonsense. Harve is a fine artist and, Harve, I'd be proud to have my work beside yours. I'm embarrassed at some of my earlier work that Mom had framed and hung up, but it was always an encouragement."

"Son, your dad did all of that."

Eric forgot his blueberry cobbler and whipped cream. "Dad did?"

"He built most of the frames and Grandma helped choose the mats."

"I didn't know that." He turned to face the others at the table. "While I was away at the Art Institute in Chicago, I had no storage space, so I'd send things home to store and the next time I'd come home, they would be beautifully matted and framed and – there was more of my work on the walls! I thought maybe it was cheaper than wall paper. I thought Mom was responsible for it." Apparently there were a lot of things about his father he hadn't known.

"Yes," his mother insisted, "and Joel just assumed that I was the one always ordering new records, or tapes. Dad would buy them and give them away and say, 'That's my singing son'."

"Did you know that, Joel?"

Joel cleared his throat. "Not until long after I moved home. Dad always gave me the dickens because I wouldn't get a *real* job."

Chapter Twenty-Five

THE MUSIC RESONATED from the converted apple warehouse into the parking lot and it was as though someone took the elbow of each of the party of four and urged them toward the building.

Earlier, Eric and Kate had met Wyn and Gwen McNeil at the Broyhill Convention Center in Boone for dinner. The restaurant was built on the top of a mountain and overlooked the campus of Appalachian State University.

"So, we look down on our alma mater. I went here to become a teacher," said Gwen.

This was one of Eric's favorite eating places, but the McNeils had never been there.

Kate was ecstatic finding one of Eric's paintings featured in the main dining room. She asked the *maitre'd* to seat them across from it. "My husband painted that picture." Eric didn't think the *maitre'd* had understood her, but a few minutes later the manager came out to greet them.

Wyn was back in boyhood form. "I grew up with Mr. Walsh, and I encouraged him to sharpen his talents. I am police officer Wyn McNeil."

The manager acknowledged each of them with a slight bow.

The painting was one of Kate's favorites. A small rural schoolhouse was showcased with the towering peaks of the Blue Ridge Mountains surrounding it. Children played Red Rover in the foreground. It was entitled, "Recess" but the name was not displayed.

Word was getting around and throughout the meal, waiters

and a few customers came to pay respects to the artist. The talented musician that had been entertaining them with music from the baby grand piano told Eric that he wished the piano faced the painting.

"We have two of Mr. Walsh's pictures, and I guess they are worth a fortune." Gwen told the pianist. She reminded Eric of his high school graduation gift to Wyn, a painting of the top of the quarry with a helicopter hovering above it. It was one of a few night scenes Eric had painted.

"I don't remember a thing about that night," Wyn said.

"I wish I didn't," Eric confessed.

Wyn drove them to the concert. His police training had been thorough and he stayed irritatingly within the speed limit, and the long drive had made them late – much to Eric's chagrin. The slow, steady rain had not helped the situation.

Eric smiled at the formal attire Wyn had arrived in, complete with vest, tie and dinner jacket, contrasting with Eric's causal plaid shirt and slacks. He had quickly removed his tie and carefully folded it before putting it into his pocket. "We're not invited to fancy places like this often," he explained. By the time they left for The Pass, Wyn had shed his vest and jacket. Gwen's flowered voile dress matched Wyn's tie. Eric glanced at Kate.

Kate complimented Gwen. "You look so pretty in red. We brought only casual clothing, but you look so right for a night out on the town!"

Gwen was a bubbly, round little woman who had talked incessantly throughout the meal and ride. She would have probably ruined the concert for them, except someone behind them hissed a loud *Shhhhh*. Eric turned around to give a thumbs up to the woman who hissed and Kate gave him a quick kick in the ankle.

It seemed a strange twist of fate that Wyn, who usually crowded everyone else out of the conversation, had married a woman who could out talk him.

Kate was a lover of serious, classical music and had a huge collection of CD's by the masters, Mendelssohn, Beethoven, Chopin and Debussy. She kept their car radio on the classical music station. Eric wasn't sure how she would react to Joel's Blue Ridge Mountain Musicmakers. He didn't need to worry. From the first note, she seemed enthralled. She leaned over to ask him to sketch the instruments.

Again, they were *shushed*. This time, Eric kept his eyes to the front.

The music reached out and grabbed them. It splashed over the audience; pulsating, filling the room with the sounds of throbbing guitars and banjos. The music spilled outside to the porch. It permeated through the audience, uniting them, filling each with toe tapping rhythm.

Eric couldn't decide which foot to tap. He noticed several people using both feet. Kate was using her right toe and heel – alternating between the two.

One, two, three, four – an explosion of guitars, banjo and drums.

The band was playing, *Whoa Mule*, featuring Lou Ann on her banjo. Then, Joel began to sing. "I went up on the mountain, to get a sack of corn." On the chorus, all the band sang:

"Whoa mule, whoa,
Whoa mule I holler"

On the last line, all the instruments were silent, except, Cleg Wiseman's who used his bow on the bass fiddle to imitate a braying mule and the audience went wild.

Tubby Tub was prominent with his wash tub. He had turned a galvanized steel wash tub over, cut a small hole in the top and strung a weed eater line to the top of a slender pole. He played it much the way the bass fiddle player strummed his instrument, plucking the string and moving his left hand up and down, tightening and loosening – raising and lowering the pitch. Sometimes, for emphasis, he lifted the whole instrument and brought it down on the floor with a bang. In other numbers, he used a wash board and accented the beat with metal thimbles on his fingers. It sounded for the world like tap dancers and the crowd loved it. Tommy also had a lovely bass voice and was featured in several solos.

Several times, on the faster music, two boys, about 10 and 12, stepped to the dance floor to clog, an incredible display of talent.

"Is this Irish dance?" Kate whispered, then stood up and moved to the side so she could watch better.

Other times, members of the audience chose partners and danced to the music.

The music and the drama of the concert captivated Eric. He shoved aside the memory of his talk with Dr. Ross following his dialysis treatment. "If you don't find a donor soon, you can measure your life in a matter of weeks."

Eric gave permission for Kate to call Clay and Dr. Young. She called Kathy also.

Tonight, he wanted to think only about coon dogs, lost loves, mountain streams and a light in the cabin window, welcoming

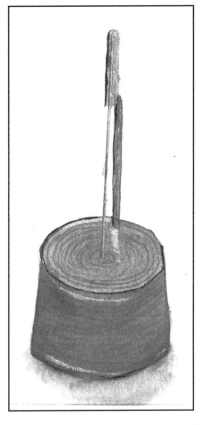

home a way-faring traveler. He experienced the magnetic pull of mountain music and a tremendous pride in his brother.

He tried to block out Kate's quiet reaction to the conversation she had with Dr. Young at the clinic this morning. She turned as pale as moonlight. He had pressed her for an explanation.

She hesitated. "I don't think it amounts to anything – but ..."

"But, what?" Could it be that after all his concerns, the doctors were going to have to reject Clay's offer?

He took Kate's hand and it was ice cold. She was trembling. "Clay has to have other tests. Dr. Young said they would inject dye into his femoral artery to check to see if there is more than one arterial branch to his kidney. Also, they have to do more blood tests and an ultrasound. They have to double-check everything and make sure he hasn't contracted some other disease since the initial testing."

Eric caressed her cheek. "Darling, don't worry. This could be God's way to tell us this is not the right path. We need every test we can find to assure us there is no danger to Clay. We can surely wait until next week," he told her, but he felt a sickening disappointment in the pit of his stomach.

"Clay is going to the hospital right now for the tests," Kate said. She gave him a brave smile but her voice was strained, abnormally high, wavering with worry.

Now, hours later, Eric tried to give his full attention to the music. What if, because of some unforeseen problems, Clay couldn't become a donor! He tried to put the brakes on his emotional roller coaster.

Bluegrass concerts often include a couple of spiritual songs and Eric glanced at his watch when Joel lead the band in *That Old Time Religion*. They had already been there an hour and a half.

Just as the band started playing *The Unclouded Day*, his cell phone began to vibrate. For a moment, he froze. Only his family members, Dr. Young and the transplant team had this number.

He edged his way toward the door praying, "Please God, let it be a donor." As he pushed open the door, he flipped the cover open to his cell phone and in a husky voice, said, "Hello?"

"Hi, Dad."

He must have had the same reaction that King Midas, of Greek mythology, had when, after praying that everything he touched would turn to gold, his darling daughter ran into his arms.

"Dad?" Clay asked.

"Hello, son." He felt weak and might have stumbled had Kate not grabbed him around the waist. Someone shoved a chair behind his legs and he slumped into it.

"It's all set, Dad. I'm in good shape. Everything is 'A OK'! Dr. Young asked me to call you. The tests checked out fine and of course they doubled-checked the other critical elements. We will both be admitted to City Hospital Monday morning. And, Dad, Jane and the kids are as enthusiastic as I am."

Eric numbly handed the phone to Kate. Their daughter-in-law had consistently supported Clay in this matter. She had once expressed the wish that she could be the donor.

"Clay," Kate explained, "your dad and I will be leaving to come home within the next couple of hours." They talked a few seconds more and Eric held his hand out for the phone.

"Thanks, son. I love you."

"I love you, too, Dad and thanks for letting me do this. This way, a part of me will be with you always."

Eric was unable to reply.

Betsy, Russell and Harve joined them on the porch. Kate explained their news. Eric asked Harve to be a substitute for him and to sketch the musicians and instruments for Kate. "She'll tell you what she wants."

The last strains of the song drifted from the concert, "And they tell me that no tears ever come again, in that lovely land of unclouded day."

Eric saw Joel signal to Snuffy to take over directing the band. Eric, watching Joel circling around the crowd, trying to get through, quickly rose to his feet. No need to alarm Joel.

"What's up?" Joel asked.

Kate answered, "Eric has a donor."

"Shall we close down right now and head for New York?"

"No," Eric said. "Don't stop. I just have to be there by Monday."

"Well, I want to introduce you, and then we usually do a little informal jamming. Give me another half hour here."

Joel took the opportunity to introduce his band members which included, in addition to the group Eric had already met, Jeb McGowen at the drums. Maggie Patter, playing a five string banjo, Babs Lunsford, mandolin, Tommy Tubs with his homemade instruments. "Also, My nephew, Al Adams, is playing guitar tonight."

"Tonight, we also have a special guest, ladies and gentlemen. I want you to meet my brother, Eric. Eric Walsh – the artist." When the applause died down, he introduced Kate. "And I see that they have brought some guests. Stand up, Officer McNeil and your lovely wife."

"And now, we have finished our planned concert, but we can

give you a little informal jamming. That's when we just play whatever comes to our heads and the songs you call out for us to play. It is your chance to be a part of the concert. Cleg, didn't you have a request? What key?"

It was the first words Eric had heard the shy bass player say. "Key of A."

They began to play *Lonesome Road Blues.*

For the next half hour the band played requests and then Joel announced, "That's all folks. I'm taking my brother to New York to get a new kidney!"

Lou Ann Puckett squealed, "Yes!" and left her place to go hug Eric. The band clapped.

Wyn and Gwen hurried to them, and Wyn wouldn't let his wife get a word in before he said, "You got the call while we were here? Way to go, Eric."

Al and Jeanne offered to ride with the McNeils to get Eric's rental car in Boone. Eric and Kate climbed into Sherie's SUV, eager to tell his mom the news and to load up for the trip North. Nothing seemed real.

Chapter Twenty-Six

His mother was crying when she held him close to whisper something into his ear as they were ready to leave. Eric smiled, patted her shoulder and said, "Bye, Mom. Joel will call you right after the surgery."

He wanted to be *gone*, and he climbed quickly into the front seat of the SUV. He leaned out the door to say, "I'm coming back to finish the grill next summer."

Kate placed a pillow under his head and Sherie inspected his seat belt. "Let's *just go*." he said. They reclined his seat until he thought his head would be in the lap of the rider in the back seat, and he protested until Kate eased in behind him. "You're fine, honey."

They were hardly out of the driveway before Joel punched him on the shoulder and asked, "What did Mom say?"

"What do you *think* she said?" Eric laughed and threw up his hands. "I could have spared myself all this grief in deciding what to do. I should have –"

"– asked Mom."

They all laughed then and Eric felt relief and joy he had been missing for a long time.

"Mom has another surprise for you, little brother. When I brought the print of Dad and Grandpa down from the attic, she insisted that I hang that in the living room. We wrapped the original *The Master Craftsman* for you."

"Why did she want to do that?"

"She said you needed it."

"Yes, I think I do. I can never forget that Dad loved me, he just didn't know how to show it. And you, Joel – he loved you and was proud of you also."

Joel nodded. "Dad was a noble man in many ways, but he just could not accept that we wouldn't – couldn't – live the same life he did. He followed his dad and expected us to do the same."

They drove down the mountain, and he could see only an outline of the Grandfather. He would try to look back at it when they reached Foscoe. He loved every angle of that mountain. There had been many angles to his problem also. He had to view it the way Kate, Kathy and Clay saw it.

Joel continued his reminiscing. "It's strange, we have been successful, both of us. I have criss-crossed the continent giving concerts and made enough money that I could come home and build a studio to record my CDs. Your work is known all over the country and when you retire, you'll spend lots of time here, painting our mountains – and Dad is not around to enjoy the family."

"I wish he was," Eric said. "We each grew up thinking we were pretty worthless. I wonder if Dad would be surprised at our successes." He felt very tired but his mind was racing. *Retire.* The young pastor had said that we were "to embrace life, to savor it and live it to the fullest." Yes! I can work for ten years, or more, and come home to retire, if I want to, *because of Clay's kidney.* "Thank you, God," he whispered, "and thank *you*, Clay, my son."

He heard Kate release her seat belt, and she leaned up to touch him on the shoulder. He loved the intimacy of her touch and he turned his head to kiss her hand.

"Sweetheart," Kate asked quietly, "you were so adamant about not taking Clay's offer. What changed your mind?"

He didn't answer immediately, but the silence in the car was amicable as though everyone understood his inability to explain logically. "I've been pretty thick-headed, granted, and it is a risk for Clay – I'd feel terrible if anything happened to him – but, my dad mattered so much to me."

"Your *dad*?" Kate asked.

"As many hard times as Dad gave me, I recognize now that he

really cared for me and I understand his hard-nosed ways. I guess that, perhaps, I feel that I'm worth the risk."

Kate raised up to kiss his forehead. "You have always been worth the risk, darling."

Joel and Sherie listened silently as Eric continued, "Clay has a part in this and I owed him the courtesy of considering his offer. In retrospect, I know what I meant to Dad, and I know what Clay

means to me. It's the only decision I could make."

Kate ruffled his hair and sank back into her seat, and Eric heard the click as she fastened her seat belt. "Do you mean that I'm going to have to put up with you another twenty or thirty years?" she teased.

Eric laughed, but he was *so sleepy*. "It's up to you if you want to put up with me, but I expect to be around a long time. Is it a bad deal for you?"

Kate choked up. "It's the only deal I ever wanted."

Sherie laughed. "Oh, you love birds!"

"I hear the violins playing," Joel said, and imitated the action of a violinist pulling the bow with his right hand.

Sherie began to sing an old mountain love song.

"Are you tired of me, darling?
Do you wish the word unsaid?
Words that made me yours forever,
On the day that we were wed."

A gentle chuckle rippled across the SUV. Eric pulled the afghan up to cover his shoulders. His mom had draped it over him just before they pulled out. A sense of contentment washed over him. Joel was driving him home, sparing him the tiresome airline travel and he felt like a pampered little brother. It felt good to be cared for.

He had made the decision he had been dreading to make and he knew it was the right one. God was faithful. He was a man at peace – with his marriage, his work; and he had come to terms with his relationship with his father. His life with Kate was better than it had ever been; and his boss in New York, although expressing a great need for him at work at the publishing house, was jubilant about the news of the donor. "Take as much time as you need, Eric."

He had come to the mountains determined to reject Clay's offer, out of his love for his son. But to do so, he would be rejecting Clay, just as he felt he had been rejected by his father.

His sleep was deep and when Joel offered a rest stop, just beyond Boone, he waved him on. Once he woke up smelling the coffee and tuna fish sandwiches his mother had prepared, but he was not interested in food or drink.

Just before daylight, they stopped in Virginia to get gas and to change drivers. The eastern sky was not quite so dark. He got out of the car to stretch his legs and he pushed himself between Kate and Sherie, put an arm around each of them and hugged them, then climbed silently back into the SUV.

As dawn painted the sky pink and a faint yellow, he woke up enough to say, "Good morning, all. And to all, good night." He snuggled back against the pillow and went back to sleep. It was the best sleep he had enjoyed in months.

The "real" wall -- built by the author and her husband at their home in Avery County.

Meet the Author:

Lila Hopkins grew up in New Mexico but, since 1992, has lived in the beautiful mountains of Western North Carolina. Her novels grow out of her love for the mountains and her admiration of the people she met in Avery County, and since 2004, her friends in Wake County.

Hopkins is the daughter of a Baptist pastor and married a Baptist minister while she was still a college student at Hardin-Simmons University in Abilene, Texas. After graduation, she taught school in northern California while her husband continued his theological studies in Berkley,California.

The Hopkins moved to North Carolina in 1960 for Rev. Hopkins to intern at the Department of Pastoral Care at Baptist Hospital in Winston-Salem. In 1961, he became chaplain at McCain Hospital, where he served for 29 years.

Lila taught school in Moore County for 13 years and the experience was the basis of her two award winning juvenile books, *Eating Crow* and *Talking Turkey*(1988 and 1990) Both books won the North Carolina Juvenile Literature Award.

Mrs. Hopkins, a watercolorist, whose paintings are featured in the Graylight Gallery in Newland, painted the dust jackets and illustrated all of her novels from Ingalls Publishing Group. *Weave Me A Song* and *Strike A Golden Chord* were each awarded Book of the Year from High Country Writers. Since 2004, she has been an columnist for the *Fuquay-Independent.*

179

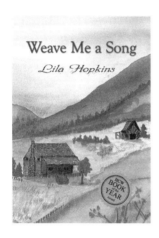

Weave Me a Song
by Lila Hopkins
illustrations by the author

ISBN: 0971304572 hardcover - $19.95

FREDDIE GOUGE returns to the Appalachians in response to an emergency call from her high school sweetheart -- her grandmother who raised her has fallen ill. Pax is now a gallery owner who displays Granny Gouge's artistic weaving. but old conflicts raise doubts.

☙

"Christian Romance with an edge – a family story of loss, betrayal and redemption." – *Mature Living, a Lifeway publication*

"Readers encounter mystery, suspense, romance, and danger. ... great summer read." – Nancy Stroupe, *The Mountain Times*

"Enchanting. . ." – *The Avery Post*

Strike a Golden Chord
by Lila Hopkins
illustrations by the author

$23.95 - ISBN: 1932158510 hardcover

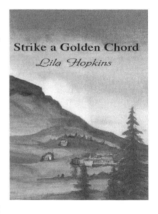

MYSTERY, intrigue, a kidnapping and a plot to steal a valuable manuscript complicate what could have been a simple romance between a church organist and an English teacher. Joanna Jerome sacrificed a concert career to care for her ailing father but finds life in Galax Falls, NC holds the potential for unexpected excitement and fulfillment.

☙

"Seamless melodious story about uncovering the hidden treasure of love. ... a book that will cause your heart to sing!" – Lynne Hinton, *Friendship Cake*

Weather of the Heart:
A Child's Journey out of Revolutionary Russia
by Nora Lourie Percival

$29.95 - ISBN: 0971304505 hardcover
$19.95 - ISBN: 0971304599 trade paperback

"Speaks for so many others who have silently endured the loss of all they valued." - Publishers Weekly

From the perspective of the 21st century, the author looks back with a clear eye to the turbulent days following the Russian Revolution. Nora Percival's research illuminates her personal story -- the story so many of us long to hear from grandparents unable or unwilling to look back beyond the immigrants' voyage to another life and another world.

Book of the Year High Country Writers org. Top six guide pick -- small press books by women writers. --About.com

Nora Percival's American life began in 1922, at the age of eight, when she was reunited with her father on Ellis Island. Her career included newspaper, magazine and book publishing, with lapses for raising five children. She worked for Random House, and for Barnard College, her alma mater, as Director of Alumnae Affairs. At the age of 92, Nora continues to write. She is an enthusiastic member of High Country Writers, regularly critiquing the work of fellow members, and editing freelance projects.

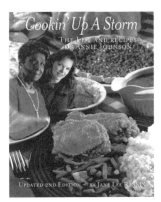

Cookin' Up A Storm
The Life and Recipes of Annie Johnson
by Jane Lee Rankin

ISBN 0965738728 trade paperback - $19.95
Grace Publishers

Jane Lee Rankin welcomes readers into the world of Annie Johnson, the family cook, teacher, lifelong friend and African American woman who introduced the author to the world of traditional Southern cooking.

📖 Marian Coe is the award-winning author of seven books, a former staffer with the St. Petersburg Times, in Florida, is an Alabama native and a transplanted North Carolinian. She lives on Sugar Mountain with her artist husband, Paul Zipperlin.

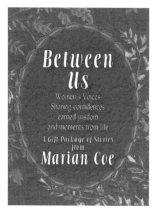

Between Us
by Marian Coe

ISBN: 1932158316, hardcover - $14.95
Southlore Press

GIFT package of shared experience from women's lives: candid, honest and personal, on a cornucopia of subjects, from shopping confessions to dealing with change. A special book to have and to give.

ଓଃ୨୦

Once Upon a Different Time
by Marian Coe
illustrations by Paul Zipperlin

$12.95 - ISBN: 1932158537 trade paperback

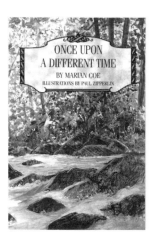

Award-winning romantic adventure based on 1880s articles in the Atlantic Monthly.

JOIN a spirited group on a romantic adventure in the Appalachian mountains in 1884, as they travel on horseback from Abingdon, Virginia to the fashionable resort of Asheville, North Carolina. Marian Coe and artist Paul Zipperlin have woven an imaginative odyssey based on the true account by Charles Dudley Warner of just such a trip published in the Atlantic Monthly of the time.

***Book of the Year: High Country Writers Organization
North Carolina Society of Historians:***

Boone: A Novel of An American Legend
by Cameron Judd

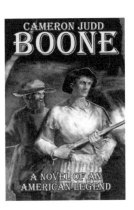

$24.95 -ISBN: 1932158685 hardcover
$16.95 - ISBN: 1932158634 trade paperback

Daniel Boone's story from this celebrated author of over forty adventure novels.

DANIEL BOONE'S LIFE was marked by destiny and contradiction. Born of Quaker stock, he was peace-loving, yet a celebrated warrior. Sympathetic to the natives of America, and in ways more like them than his own people, he became trailblazer for the aggressive white civilization. Devoted to family, he spent long months apart, leaving his resilient wife to fend for herself and their children. Inclined by temperament to mind his own affairs, he was called into leadership and responsibility at every phase of his life. In this recounting of the most pivotal years of the Boone legend, author Cameron Judd interweaves the facts of Daniel Boone's life and destiny with a story crafted from history and shaped by imagination.

IPPY Honor Book 2006
Winner: Wilma Dykeman Award for Regional Fiction

ଓଞ୨୦

MAGGIE BISHOP writes mystery and romantic suspense set in the Appalachians. She uses friends and local personalities as characters, but "the murders are all made up." She's an Air Force brat who put herself through East Carolina University, a former manufacturing executive, founder of High Country Writers and a hiker, swimmer, golfer and a skier.

Chosen in 2007 as one of 100 Incredible ECU Women for her literary and leadership works

Murder at Blue Falls
An Appalachian Adventure Mystery
$12.00 – trade paperback ISBN: 9781932158755

We hope you've enjoyed this very special book from
High Country Publishers &
INGALLS PUBLISHING GROUP, INC

We invite you to peruse the preceeding pages of descriptions of other fine works of fiction and memoir from
INGALLS PUBLISHING GROUP.

More books and ordering information are available on our website:

www.ingallspublishinggroup.com

INGALLS PUBLISHING GROUP, INC